DAMAGED

MUHAMMAD ALI SAMEJO

Printed in the Islamic Republic of Pakistan.
Printed: November, 2020
Edition: 1st
ISBN: 978-969-749-016-5
Price: Rs 1200 PKR, $12 US

ISLAMABAD, PAKISTAN

raabta@auraqpublications.com | +92-300-0571-530
www.auraqpublications.com | @AuraqPublications

ISBN : 978-969-749-016-5

DEDICATION

To my father, Muhammad Bakhsh Samejo. None of this would have been possible without your love, your devotion, and for being the greatest dad who ever lived.

To my two moms, Shamim Shahnaz Samejo and Suraiya Solangi. You're the blueprint for loving mom-and-aunt duos everywhere and I'm ever so grateful that you're mine.

To my siblings, Ahmed, Mustafa and Kainat. You're the best friends I could have ever asked for and God bless you all.

To my wife Roshna, and my girls Eva and Zeest. Thanks for bringing a ton of happiness to my life.

To Amna, Sababa and Hafsa. If it weren't for you reminding me that I loved reading so much, I would never have ventured into something like this. At all!

To Nazia Kamran Kashif, and all of the fine people at the Pakistan Artists, Bloggers, Writers, Readers and Poets. Thank you so much for letting me be a part of your wonderful family.

To everyone who I haven't been able to mention here... you know who you are. And you're awesome!

'damaged'
/ˈdamɪdʒd/
verb
past tense of 'damage' /ˈdamɪdʒ/

'inflict harm so as to impair its value, usefulness, or normal function.'
'have a detrimental effect on.'

Contents

01

POWER

Alamgir wakes up with a splitting headache, groaning as his eyes try to acclimatize to the lights. He attempts to gather his bearings while at the same time hoping to recall just what happened to him. More importantly, figure out where on earth he is. His eyes adjust to the bright lights beaming down from an indiscernible source above, and he's surrounded by glass all around him.

He feels the transparent but thick walls around him as he takes stock of the limited space that he's inside. Darkness prevails outside the glass as only his little six-by-six chamber seems to be engulfed in light.

Not exactly a glass chamber. A cage.

"Try to remember, please try to remember..."

He looks at his grey suit, the one he wore to the party the night before. At least he *thinks* it was the night before. He can't remember where it was, or which one. Checking his pockets to find no cell phone, wallet, car keys, not even his fresh-breath spray, he can't help but groan. Curiously enough, he's also missing his wrist watch, trouser belt and his shoes of all things. He touches his face to feel the stubble growing. So *when* is the next question on his mind. Leading to the next one: how long.

"That's how it feels, you know."

He turns to face the voice of the woman approaching him, still giving him no clue as to which direction she's coming from. There's no opening behind her, no doorway or light source to indicate that she came from another room. He can only see her silhouette approaching from the brief glints of light from his own chamber, her hair straightened with a touch of brown, her body dressed in a formal shirt and pants, a handbag slung on her shoulder as she wheels a small office chair towards the cage before finally seating herself on it. Alamgir takes a good look at her and could have just chuckled, were it not for the fact that he has absolutely no idea what's going on.

"What is this?" He finally asks.

"Can't you tell?" She counters back, folding her arms.

"How did I get here? Did you bring me here?"

"Flunitrazepam."

"What?"

"Oh right," she replies, "you would probably know it as Rohypnol. You know, the same pill you use all the time with your little *conquests*. The same one you used with me. So now you know how much the headaches hurt. Just like the one I felt the next morning after you..."

At hearing this, Alamgir finally chuckles.

"Is that what this is about?" He asks, nonchalantly.

"So you don't deny it?"

"What's there to deny?" He replies. "It's not some closely guarded big secret, though no one has ever been able to prove anything and neither have any of them come forward. Certainly not you, Sarah."

On hearing her name, Sarah is caught off guard completely for the first time, showing a bit of a chink in her armor.

"Oh what, you think I don't remember you?" Alamgir stands confident as he leans his arm along the glass cage. "I remember them all, Sarah. I've even got an album, you know."

"You destroyed my life," Sarah utters, obviously trying to hold back the lump in her throat.

Alamgir just scoffs and walks around a little in his cage.

"No, Sarah. It was you who was about to destroy your life. And may I add with total disregard for your own self."

"What are you talking about?"

"You know, when I first met you at work, like *really* met you for the first time, do you know what I felt? Would you care to know?"

Sarah stares at him, her folded arms tightening their grip around her.

"Nothing. Absolutely nothing."

"That's rich!" Sarah scoffs now, rolling her head in sync with her eyes.

"I mean, how can you feel about another human being out of a population of billions? Sure you looked cheerful and smart and maybe even have been good company in bed if I had put my mind to it. Full disclosure, I hadn't. But then we started working closely together and that's when I began to admire you."

Sarah chuckles sarcastically and shakes her head, not believing what she's hearing.

"No really, see. Here was a woman who knew what she wanted out of her life. A career trajectory taking her to all new heights, and you had the tenacity to get what you wanted to add to your professional credentials. How could I not admire that? That's why you and I gelled so well together, why our projects would always be the ones that got the best output, why our two heads were better than the entire floor."

He looks down at his shoes as he puts his hands in his trouser pockets.

"Which is why I was disappointed so much with you."

Sarah cocks her head, her face bearing an expression of cluelessness, one that Alamgir doesn't fail to notice.

"See, that's exactly the look I had! I could not believe it when you told me you were going to leave everything - the job, the career, the prospects - everything just so you could go off and get married. That everything you had accomplished so far was probably just so you could make yourself more marketable in some demented bride market. That you were just working so you could save enough money to pay for wedding celebrations, a few days of pleasing two different extended families and save your old man some grief about expenses, becoming some other guy's financial burden because obviously no self-respecting groom would *allow* his wife to work. Not in this country, anyway."

Unable to hear any more, Sarah quickly stands up and stands close to the cage.

"You bastard!" She screams. "You total bastard! You ruined my life, you ruined my future! When the police found me in the streets and I was examined at the hospital, the groom's family wanted nothing to do with me anymore. They made it all public, about what happened to me. He…"

She takes a moment to wipe away her tears that she couldn't hold back any longer.

"He wouldn't even stand to look at me. To him, I was worse than a leper."

Alamgir examines Sarah huffing and puffing from behind the glass, poised to break through and even hurt him. He calculates his steps as he walks up to the side of the glass where she's standing, his hands still in his pocket.

"Ruined? Me? No, you're not listening to me. *You* were the one ruining it. You were the one who was about to throw away everything you had worked so hard for. You were destined for great things, Sarah, but you just got blinded in this stupid little notion this country has of just settling down, having a husband and taking care of a house full of total strangers. And for what? Haven't you realized the truth of it all? Once they realized you were, well, *used* goods, they wanted to be rid of you."

Sarah scoffs again, her arms folded now.

"No, they didn't stop there," Alamgir continues. "They made it their business to ruin you publicly. This matter could have just remained between your families, but they didn't want that. Oh no, they had to tell everyone and their maids the whole thing. *That's* what ruined you. People, fickle people. So no, I did not ruin anything for you. If anything, I set you free."

"Set me free?" Sarah retorts. "You call this freedom? My parents suffer constantly under the shadow of what happened to me, of what I am now. They worry about what will happen to me, about my future. No family wants a rape victim as a daughter-in-law. If anything, they point fingers and question what happened to me. That I'm not a victim but whatever happened to me was... consensual."

"Oh isn't that just the most rotten cliché there could be! 'She was working, she must have had male colleagues, she must have been sneaking around one. These career girls these days are completely characterless!'"

Sarah doesn't answer, merely fumes.

"I know I'm right." Alamgir chuckles. "And that's what you want? A life of unending verbal abuse, till eventually they kick you out of the house, another broken woman out of a broken marriage working in some primary school. Tell me *that* future is so rosy compared to what you were doing at the firm."

It's Sarah's turn to pace around the empty hall outside in the darkness as she takes a moment to calm herself.

"Look at you!" Sarah turns around to face him, gritting her teeth and almost foaming at the mouth. "So sure of yourself; cocky, arrogant. You think you can justify yourself with all that and feel no remorse or shame about it."

"How," Alamgir scratches his forehead, "how did you even find out it was me? I don't leave any evidence, ever. No one ever remembers seeing me."

"It would never have occurred to me it would be you," Sarah replies. "You were such..."

She laughs suddenly, choking as she holds back her tears.

"... you were such a sweet person, at least that's what I had always thought. To think you could have done this to me - or to anyone else, or *at all* - was inconceivable. But then someone came to me, someone who also suffered because of you. She told me about all of it: what you did to her and me, your lifestyle, how you charmed women and got them into parties, how you managed to break through their defenses one by one till finally making your move. I couldn't believe it at first. I was so distraught emotionally that I couldn't think straight. She persisted but I didn't believe her. Couldn't believe it was you."

"Thank... you?" Alamgir grins sarcastically.

"But then," she continues, "I started piecing everything that happened to me, going back in reverse and going back to what happened, what we did once I told you about my marriage. And once I realized it after she told me everything, all I could think about was your stupid, stupid perfume: that musky odor you would always have. I thought about it when I was shivering on the cold examination table, when they were taking swabs of DNA from me. And now when I remember that event, all I can think of in between those shivers that I smelled of your perfume, that stupid perfume. I smelled of *you*. Every time I touch my neck now, all I can feel is your breath on it. All I can hear are your groans when you..."

"Caught out by a dream," Alamgir smirks. "That's original."

"Shut up when I'm talking!" Sarah bangs the glass again. "You have no idea what it feels like! Your sounds, your breath, and that damned smell! All that's in my head right now is how you violated me entirely, and then left me on the streets like garbage."

"It was near a medical center. There was a mosque nearby, and people would have been coming out for *Fajr* prayer to go to their homes. That's all because I cared for you."

"Stop! Justifying! Yourself!" She bangs the glass after every word as her tears return. "You do *not* get to be in control, not today. And you do not care, not one bit. Not for me, and certainly not for the others you've been destroying all your life."

"Oh Sarah," Alamgir is yet to break a sweat considering he's being held prisoner against his will. "You don't have an inkling of what I do or why I do it. You're assuming that every one of my..."

Alamgir looks at the floor, as he rubs his temples with his fingers.

"... okay, let's call them *victims* if it makes you feel any better. Did you know at least half of them were practically asking for it? With their stupid little charades of how they wanted to have companionship or be in a relationship, to be loved and swooned and pampered and yadda yadda yadda!"

On hearing this, Sarah stands with her mouth agape.

"Oh don't look so surprised, you know I'm right. Back in the day, guys would be so hard-pressed to just getting women's phone numbers, they'd have to resort to getting them off of easy-load vendors. And now? Now it's like women are practically distributing them en masse. This age of social media, Insta-whatever, multiplexes, coffee shops and your average gender enlightenment is just an easy means of mingling and getting to know each other. 'Ooh let's hang out, how about that new sushi place, God you are such a tease...' seriously, it's like you lot are all practically holding neon sign boards begging to be fucked! I mean, you all still think the guys you're so trusting of are just content with keeping it all platonic. Pathetic, really."

"That's disgusting!"

"No, I'll tell you what's *actually* disgusting. Teenagers who are hitting puberty waiting in line at some amusement park, patting each other, holding hands and going on and on about relationships, sexual innuendo, and just how much it would cost to get their assignments done by the nerds. Yeah, apparently that's a thing too. There are like four or five girls and a single guy who's got this stupid smile on his face now that he's surrounded by something he can't fully understand or believe. He's got a hard-on he tries his best to hide but those girls know it, no matter how dim the lighting is. All these kids on their phones making plans to ditch school and *chilling* at someone's place. Kids who have the

Kama Sutra on their phone screens and are discussing the kind of positions any of them wouldn't be caught dead in, or otherwise."

"You truly have a filthy mind!" Sarah retorts. "But then, that's you. You look for the worst in everything, and your mindset can't comprehend any of it."

"Keep telling yourself that, but deep down, you know I'm right. Teenagers shouldn't be swooning over whatever their hormones keep pushing them to. They need to focus, they need to be better. They've got all of adult life to be *woke*."

"There you are again: justifying yourself. Slithering like the snake you are. That's all you're doing right now. You can try and sugar coat it all you like, but in the end you're just a monster plain and simple. You don't care what you do or who you destroy. You're the worst kind of monster, the kind that preys on the innocent. Like those barbarians who prey on little children."

The cocky smile leaves Alamgir's face for the first time and is replaced by a furious scowl as he narrows his eyes.

"You dare?" Alamgir barely sounds audible and then rages on towards the glass, banging it intently. "You... dare?!"

Sarah recoils just a bit till she is assured the thick glass will hold steady.

"You think I'm anything like those... no, no, no; I am *nothing* like them! I would never harm a child, a child with so much optimism in those eyes, who knows nothing about what the world is really like till they find out. And what's been happening to these kids on the news is just monstrous! But to accuse me of something like that... I swear I would strangle you right now if I could."

"Seriously?" Sarah is smiling now. "You draw a line? *You?* Unbelievable!"

"What's not to believe? What kind of a human being do you think I am?"

"Oh I don't think you're any kind of human being at all."

"No, you don't get to judge me. You said I was the one who thought the worse out of everything, well what do you suppose you're doing right now? You're putting me alongside people who are so sick and twisted that nothing is sacred to them. I mean, there's an entire organized ring of predators stalking little kids working in mines for God's sake! Or what's happening in seminaries or school vans. Oh no, I abhor everything that happens to those poor little children. And those monsters? They're the ones who deserve this - whatever this is - not me!"

"Are you actually making a case for yourself based on this?" Sarah shakes her head as she leans forward. "You are a predator. One of the vilest creatures there can be. You pick someone helpless, you take away their will, their dignity, violate their most sacred possessions: their selves. You don't care who you hurt, who you destroy, what havoc you wreak upon their lives. It doesn't matter if you do it to me or other women, or to children. Just because you think you draw a line doesn't absolve you of your crimes."

Sarah leans forward as she continues.

"But here's something else I've discovered about you. You think you did what you did to me because you wanted to teach me a lesson. You might have had similar reasons for the others. But deep down, you know you do this just because you can. Because you know no one would ever stop you, or find out about you, or report you. You have a certain method by which you avoid detection, sure, but even if your victims knew about you, you're content by the fact that no one would do anything to stop you. Well, until now anyways."

With that, Sarah gets up from the chair and begins to walk away slowly.

"Wait, so that's it?" Alamgir calls back. "You're just going to put me in a box and leave? You are coming back, aren't you?"

"Why?" Sarah doesn't turn around but stops in her steps. "Why should I?"

"Well come on! This place isn't exactly meant for comfort, you know. You must have thought this through. A guy's gotta shit, shower and shave! And food? I'm getting something to eat, aren't I? Every prison gives this much to the inmates."

Sarah laughs, for the first time as she walks back towards the glass cage.

"You don't get it, do you?" Sarah speaks between the laughter. "You're not leaving. You're *never* leaving. This is it for you. There is no escape and certainly no comfort for the likes of you. Personally, I don't know what's going to happen to you because quite frankly, I'm never coming back."

"Hehehe, look at you." Alamgir chuckles. "Is this your way to cope? To show that you can punish me?"

"No, you still don't get it. You see, I meant it when I said you're not going anywhere. This little cell is where it ends for you. I could have had you tied up in there and bludgeoned you to death, but deep down I knew it would still give you the satisfaction of being in control. Of dictating to me what you wanted done. But now? Now I've taken away your power, your sense of control over the world. Now, you're just going to stew in here in your own filth with no chance of getting out. There's nothing in there that'll help you escape. And maybe, just maybe, the next person you were about to violate last night would have another chance to lead a normal life, and the next, and the next, and the next."

"Sarah... dear, dear Sarah," Alamgir looks at her, uncertain what to expect, "you can't leave me in here because quite honestly, you don't have it in you."

Her eyes boiling in rage, Sarah grins at him one last time.

"Yes, the Sarah you knew didn't have it in her. But the one you created, the one you left behind in that street, the one you turned me into certainly can."

"You won't get away with this!" Alamgir is finally beginning to sweat from the forehead.

"Maybe. But you won't either. Good bye."

Sarah wheels the office chair back into the darkness, ignoring the pleas and screams from Alamgir and the noise he makes as he tries to punch and break the thick bulletproof glass panes. He continues, as Sarah's silhouette disappears completely.

02

FAME

Sherry jumps out of his sleep, though he regrets it instantly as the pain begins to sear right through his whole body. His screams don't exactly exit entirely in full volume from his mouth, muffled behind the bandages surrounding his entire face and head. The screams die down, only to be replaced by panicked panting as Sherry tries to check his face and is horrified to discover the bandages. Naturally one doesn't do such a thing to oneself, so it doesn't take long for him to determine that there seems to be a gap between now and the last time he had his eyes open.

Which was... when exactly?

He knows who he is, that much is a relief. He remembers he was out somewhere, driving through the day to a friend's place for a party. Or a retreat? Some kind of event that seems to be escaping his memory. He doesn't seem to remember much else, as he tries to get an idea of his surroundings.

At once, he is attracted to something warm. The small slits in his bandages where his eyes are help him to see a glowing warm fire. The warm LED lamps around the room also shed light on a cozy brown interior with basic furniture, a rug, a coffee table in between and some books on a shelf. He tries to get up from the sofa cum bed he lay on and discovers the pain continues to torment him from head to toe. Trying to catch his breath from the effort, he tries to speak but his words come out muffled.

"Easy there."

Barely able to turn his neck, Sherry's field of vision registers the figure hove into view a few seconds after he heard the words. The voice was masculine and sure enough, the man stood in front of him, bending over the coffee table to put down a tray. The stranger then crouches in front of Sherry to face him directly.

"Yeah, apparently I used up a lot of the dressing. Hold on."

The man turns back to the tray and holds up a pair of scissors.

"Don't move. I'll try to make this more comfortable."

Sherry sits petrified, not sure what to expect next. The stranger carefully brings the scissors near Sherry's mouth, cutting up enough of the bandage to make it easier for him to speak and move his jaw. He does the same for his eye slits and nose, taking care not to poke his skin.

"Apologies for the discomfort. I'm not very good at this."

Sherry attempts to lick his lips and exert a bit more control at his jaw.

"W... w... wat...er..."

"Oh, yes of course."

The stranger brings up a glass of water and gently wets Sherry's lips before giving him small sips.

"Slowly, now. You haven't had anything for hours now. I'll get you some soup in a little bit if you feel up to it."

"Whhh... where..." Sherry attempts to ask "Where am... I?"

"My cabin in the woods. I found you on the road."

"My... car?"

"There was an accident. You were lucky you weren't inside it before it caught fire and exploded. It looked like a new model, so you should have put your seatbelt on."

"What?"

"I'm guessing your car had airbags. They don't work if you don't put your seatbelt on. The crash was bad, and you were hurled right out of your windscreen. Your face..."

Sherry begins to burn a hole right through his eye slits.

"What... what about my face?" he manages to ask.

"Oh don't worry, nothing too bad.... I think. There are a lot of cuts and bruises on one side, but nothing too serious. I've tried to put on as much medication as I could, but it'll take time for you to heal."

"No, it's not possible!" Sherry's voice is full of despair now. "This can't be happening to me."

"I'm sorry. I get that you must be in shock."

"My phone! Did you find my phone?"

The stranger narrows his brow and walks to the other side of the room. He returns and drops two objects next to Sherry.

"Your wallet managed to survive, but the phone wasn't that lucky. Anyways, there's no cell reception up here."

"Do you have anything to help me contact someone? A phone, Internet?"

"Sorry, I don't really have anything that can help you."

"Seriously?" Sherry scoffs under the bandages somehow. "You're telling me you don't have a laptop or broadband?"

"I did mention this is a cabin in the woods, didn't I? The phone company didn't think it wise to expand up here. Not enough clients, they said."

"You've got lights, electricity." Sherry retorts.

"Solar and batteries. I don't use much. Off-the-grid living at its finest."

As Sherry's eyes are getting accustomed to the setting around him, he gets a good look at his host who now seats himself on the couch across from him. Long hair and a beard that made it appear as if his host was saving on his shaving expenses. To Sherry, he looked like a hermit in every sense of the word, right down to the cabin in the woods with a fireplace. And while Sherry didn't realize it at first, it would appear even to the most casual observer that the hermit had the feeling he was being laughed at by his guest.

"Are you for real?" Sherry continues to ponder in disbelief. "No phone, no computer, no TV even?"

"Scary, huh?" the hermit chuckles.

"So, you don't know who I am then."

"No," the hermit raises an eyebrow. "Should I?"

"Hehehe..." Sherry can't help but laugh. "That has got to be a first. I'm known as Sherry. I'm a Vlogger."

"Okay..." the hermit's eyebrow keeps inclining and curving beyond its limit. "Pardon my ignorance, but do you mind clearing up what that is? It doesn't seem like it has anything to do with trees."

"What?" Sherry asks in amazement.

"Vlogger, logs?"

"Dude, no!" Sherry tries to slap his palm but the effort strains him.

"Easy!" The hermit almost gets up, prompting Sherry to gesture him not to.

"No, uh..." Sherry continues, "You're a long ways off. I'm talking about making videos for YouTube!"

"You... tube. Oh, I know that one. Didn't they ban it years ago?"

"What?!" Sherry exclaims. "Where have you been the last ten years?"

"Well, *here*. Obviously."

"Ten years?" Sherry tries to look amazed as much as he can while having his face obscured by bandages. "You still think Youtube is banned?"

"Something about blasphemy, if memory serves. Though I think there were deeper political and social reasons."

"Man, you're ancient by today's standards," Sherry continues to smile underneath his bandages, finding his humor back. "That's like history today. YouTube is life now, and I'm one of many Pakistani Vloggers out there. One of the most successful ones, anyway."

"I see." The hermit nods in quiet contemplation, though to Sherry, it may have appeared as if he were in awe of him.

"I have a following of like over a million subscribers, and my videos have around a hundred million views."

The hermit whistles. "That's a lot. Subscribers? So they pay you."

"Well, YouTube does!" Sherry replies emphatically. "I'm making quite a good amount of money, and so are many, many more."

"At such a young age?"

"It's the age of the youth, bro." Sherry almost starts to preach. "Social media is giving us all avenues to be successful and have a voice around the world. Those millions upon millions of views include an international audience too."

"Indeed. For a second there, I thought the Internet had reached a great deal of the country's population."

"Oh it has, that's why there are so many young people contributing on social media like Instagram, Snapchat, YouTube and you name it."

"Right," the hermit shakes his head. "Sorry, don't know any of those other ones."

"You do remember Facebook though, right?" Sherry snickers.

"Please." The hermit cocks his head.

"Thank God for that."

"So, what do you do on Youtube?" The hermit continues to pose questions. "I mean, with all those views, do you make compelling entertainment?"

"Oh yeah, sure!" Sherry answers proudly. "We friends get together, hang out, chill, play video games and travel some, go around town, record everything we do. We've got some talented people who make the videos so aesthetically appealing that we have such a huge following."

"So basically, you're a modern version of Seinfeld?"

"What?"

"Right, that would be before your time."

"I could Google it if my phone was in one piece."

"Ah, I remember that one."

Sherry continues to shake his head in disbelief, or as much as he can without grimacing in pain.

"Bro, how old are you?" He asks his host.

"Thirty-nine," the hermit replies. "Turning forty next April."

"Damn, bro! I could do a whole show on you."

"I'd rather you didn't."

"No, I mean it." Sherry leans a bit forward, his elbows on his knees now. "You have no idea how fascinated people will be with your story. You are truly something *dope* in this day and age. And imagine the amount of people your story would reach thanks to me."

"Thanks to you?"

"Well, duh bro!" Sherry continues. "I told you, right? I'm an influencer."

"Is it what I think it means?"

"And more!" Sherry continues proudly. "Everyone out there on Instagram or Youtube these days is an Influencer. Our content is what the youth tunes into, and we deliver to them what they need. Entertainment, jokes, humor, restaurant reviews. And naturally with it comes the opportunity for corporates to sell their stuff. We're like official spokespeople for them now, and our role as Influencers means the Internet is now a formidable medium for marketing too."

"Sounds... tedious."

Sherry's bandages make it hard for the hermit to determine his expressions, but the scoff can only mean that he is flabbergasted at the comment.

"Well, I don't expect you to understand," Sherry retorts, "what with your lifestyle and everything. But what I do is more than tedious. It is back-breaking hard work. Working week in and week out to remain on top, making sure the number of subscribers and views keeps increasing, remaining at the cutting edge of content because let's face it, there are way too many Youtubers out there and they are hungry to take out the big fish."

"Like you?"

"Especially like me! I'm one of the pioneers, and the youth love me. I've been told just what a huge change I've brought about in their lives, and how they've said no to the path that was pre-decided for them by their parents. Now they want to follow their dreams and do something creative."

"Like you?"

"Yeah, mostly all of them think about going into Social Media influencing. I say, more power to them, but it's a struggle. Not everyone is cut out for this, you know."

"Right. So presumably, you help them out?"

"What, no! I mean, not yet anyways."

"Yet?"

"I mean, I'm a busy guy, bro. I hardly have the time from my own projects to help others with theirs. It's not an easy thing, you know. I didn't get all the way to the top because someone held my hand and helped me along the way."

"So you're never going to give back, then?"

"I never said that!" Sherry sounds defensive now. "Maybe someday. But I give back in my own way. We do stuff for charity every now and then. Making videos about social issues and ills prevalent in society."

"Ah, now that is noble. Why didn't you say so?"

"Excuse me?" Sherry inquires.

"Well it stands to reason with the amount of reach and subscribers you have, you could definitely be an agent for change. I'm sure your videos must focus on the problems our country faces, and of course create awareness on how to counteract them, right?"

In the silence, the sounds of the fire burning in the fireplace creates a serene atmosphere, as Sherry wonders at the comments of his host. If there were a bowl containing quiet contemplation, it appears as if it has been passed on to Sherry to partake from.

"I... that is... well, we do but not so much. That's not the kind of content we make. We're a youth channel, and my focus is primarily on the youngsters of today making the best for themselves. Getting more experiences, refreshing their minds, breaking the shackles of tradition, becoming more *woke*."

"Woke?"

"It's slang these days for being aware. Of knowing how the system holds you down."

"Right. And like you mentioned, it also allows for you to sell something to them on behalf of the corporates that sponsor you."

"Oh great, here we go!" Sherry raises his arms in disbelief as much as he can without causing too much pain. "Just because I've got some good sponsors doesn't mean I'm a sellout, bro. It just means they value my... well... value."

"I see." The hermit sounds skeptical. "Well I suppose it doesn't matter if you help out small businesses every now and then. I'm sure you could spare that much."

"Right. Yeah." Sherry answers half-heartedly.

And as the raging fire occupies the silence for another minute or so while the hermit sits on his couch and contemplates, Sherry decides to act more defensive again.

"Hey, don't you judge me! You don't even know me or the struggles I've been through. I have worked so hard, sacrificed so much to be where I am today. And yeah, maybe my priorities could be a bit more altruistic. But it's not like they aren't. I'm certainly better than most other Youtubers out there. Definitely better than that hack Freddy!"

"Freddy who?"

"This other expat Youtuber who is way past his prime. He started off great and had better reach because he lived abroad, and because of his girlfriend slash wife slash business partner Diva."

"That's her real name, is it?"

"Divya, actually. But yeah, they were the gold standard before they started becoming so irrelevant that they had to go through cheap tricks like pretending to get married and then revealing they weren't. That got them a lot of views, sure, but it also got them tons of hate too. They call him *Frauddy* now because of all the lame and fake stunts they have pulled to attract attention."

"Heh, Frauddy. Very clever." The hermit smirks. "And I take it you don't appreciate them either?"

"Oh, now that's different. Because I'm the one who's taken their throne and spot as the number one Youtuber in Pakistan. I'm the one who people flock to now because I tell the truth. Those two haven't been the same after I exposed them all those years ago, and people are now more *woke* about them because of me. But rather than accept defeat, those two started harassing me on social media and started making videos trying to discredit me. But I showed them, ha!"

"Let me get this straight." The hermit leans forward now. "You're trying to tell me your popularity has soared largely because of this feud you have going on with someone else who does similar work to yours, and now both of you are in some kind of ratings war?"

"Call it what you like," Sherry responds. "But those two are a joke, and people can see that clearly now thanks to me. Hehe, it's so bad that those two had to come back here to Pakistan to win their self-respect and fans back. They even had this grand party at this hill station around here."

"Oh right," the stranger rubs his chin, "the one that's not too far from the road you were on. Is that where you were returning from?"

Sherry is about to answer when he suddenly realizes what has just happened As if the blurred picture in his head starts to become clearer.

"Yeah, yeah... you're right. That's *exactly* where I was. I was at this party those two hosted up here, and they even had the nerve to call in other Youtubers. None of them were happy to be there, and those two were just rubbing shoulders with everyone and trying to get some *selfies* in."

"Selfies?"

"Oh God, it's like I'm back in the stone-age with you! Just think of photos, tons of photos. And... and... Yeah, *now* I remember! It was also supposed to be an event where some major corporate client was supposed to be meeting me. They wanted me to do their content development on Youtube, but somehow those two got to know about it. That's why they wanted to have this party! So Frauddy and

Diva could schmooze my client out from right under my nose. And they had the nerve to do it right in front of everyone."

"That is pretty underhanded of them."

"You think! And when I called them out on it, they went off on me right at my face. Things got pretty heated, I said a lot of things I'm not proud of and then I just drove off. Those two got under my skin so bad, I just wanted to get away from there. I didn't even want to go there in the first place but the other Influencers insisted I let bygones be bygones, for all the good it did me."

"You were driving very fast, I take it." The hermit states it more like a question.

"Yeah, I just wanted to get out of there, and then the maps in my car went offline for some reason. I tried to slow down but..."

At that instant, it's almost as if a light bulb goes off inside Sherry's head, shedding more light on the clearing picture.

"What?"

"Oh those motherfuckers!"

"Excuse me?"

"Those two, they set the whole thing up! They wanted me to come over to the party. They wanted me to get infuriated over there and leave in a huff. They planned this whole thing out to get me to drive off at a fast rate of speed, just so I could lose control and get into an accident. And do you want to know how they would be sure I would?"

"I think I'm getting there."

"They fixed my car's brakes to fail. They made sure I ... oh my God! They tried to kill me!"

With this massive reveal, the hermit holds his head in his hands for Sherry to just stare at him.

"That's a very... very bold assumption..."

"Oh come on, you know damn well that's what happened. Those two hate me so much that they would rather see me dead than to stand in their way. This is *so* like them! They think by killing me they'll just bring out the crocodile tears and take over my spotlight? Well, they have no idea who they're dealing with! I'm far stronger than they know."

"You're not seriously suggesting they had something to do with your accident."

"Oh yeah!" Sherry guffaws, becoming rather animated under his bandages. "Well, wait till the police and press don't find a body in my car! We'll see the look on their faces then."

At this, the hermit rises from his chair and walks towards a chest of drawers on another side of the room. Opening one of the drawers and then closing it, he brings a piece of paper measuring six inches by two and three-quarters, and holds it for Sherry to take.

"And what is this supposed to be?" Sherry asks the hermit, sounding assertive but caught off-guard just a little.

"Your check."

"What?" Sherry sounds completely confused now. "What check?"

"The one you gave me because I wouldn't accept an electronic transfer. For services rendered."

Sherry continues to look even more surprised at the hermit, who just rolls his eyes at his guest's cluelessness.

"You honestly don't remember, do you?"

"Remember what?"

"Do you think the reason you had an accident is because your rivals wanted you dead?"

"You've got a better explanation?"

"No. What I have is the *truth*. And the truth is you had the accident because that's what *you* wanted to happen."

"What the fuck are you talking about?"

"Oh come on, are you this dense? It was *you*, Sherry! You paid me to tamper your brakes to make it look like they were tampered. You concocted this whole crazy scheme to get into an accident and have me remove you from there. You had me bring you here so you could rest a few days and then get back to civilization, marking it as the biggest comeback in the history of Youtube. And then you'd give press conferences and hurl accusations at your rivals for trying to have you killed and what-not."

"No, that's not true!" Sherry tries to get up but discovers the pain won't allow him to stand up without grimacing."

"Take the check."

With deep, long breaths and his heart beating intensely enough for him to register every single beat in his head, Sherry takes the check from the hermit, his hand shaking as he makes out his handwriting and signature for an amount of half a million rupees. He holds it by the tip of his fingers as the synapses in his brain begin to fill in the missing gaps inside his memory. Upon realizing the hermit was speaking the truth, he begins to cry inside his bandages and tries to cover his eyes with his other hand.

"It'll be dawn soon. I'll take you to the nearby police station in the morning, they know me there. I'll tell them I found you near the wreckage of your car and patched you up. As for the rest, you can decide on your own. I'll get you some soup. Eat up, and never come back to my house again."

As the hermit begins to walk away, Sherry continues to cry as he calls him one more time.

"Wait, please." Sherry chokes up as he asks. "Just who are you?"

With his back turned, the hermit replies.

"Someone who got tired of humanity a long time ago and didn't want anything to do with it. You came to me because you found out I lived here and could help you out. I only took your check because I didn't think you would actually go ahead with this whole thing. But you proved me wrong, horribly wrong. And also proved that the decision I made ten years ago still holds true. No matter what time you live in, or how enlightened your society continues to get, everyone out there just wants to be the one everyone else will follow. Oh and of course, everything's going to be okay, just as long as you have money to throw."

At the sound of birds beginning their morning song some time before the sunrise, the hermit walks into the kitchen space to stir a pot on the stove, while Sherry continues to sob and sniffle as he crumples the check in his fist.

<u>03</u>

BLIGHT

Walking down the dimly lit staircase toward her destination, the woman wearing the white lab coat and her head covered in a traditional headscarf - that shows only her forehead and face - looks steadily ahead at her path. A calm but nervous expression prevails over her, and her anxiety rises just a little when the door to the stairs behind her closes. Nevertheless, she buries down her fears in the pit of her subconscious as her face turns to the quality of stone. Even as she approaches the bars of the cell, she can only gulp her gasp at the sight that awaits her.

With only one light bulb shining over the chair at a considerable distance outside the cell, she sits down as her hand goes for something below her neck and hidden underneath her *dupatta*. A rattle from it makes it sound like a metal pendant. But the minute sound of it awakens another behind the bars. With only the moonlight casting an ethereal light inside the cell, she can see clearly the man sitting inside in the lotus position, his upper body naked and gleaming gray from the moonlight shining through the little barred window. He appears to be wearing only a pair of tattered trousers and no shoes. His hair is overgrown and unkempt, his beard unruly and mixing with his hair, with hints of gray, black and white blended together. His frame is skinny and his torso seems to have his ribs protruding outwards. His wrists have shackles, but the chains that were supposed to be joining them together seem to have been broken right at the middle. On another side of the cell, she sees a pile of white rags gathering dust.

At the sound of her pendant rattling, she is briefly startled at the prisoner shifting inside, his head full of overgrown and unkempt long hair turning just enough for her to notice the gleam of his eye from behind the hair. She realizes he is scrutinizing her just as intensely as she is; though both of them keep their feelings subdued enough from changing the looks on their faces.

"Are you lost, child? There are no bathrooms down here. Perhaps you should inquire from one of the guards."

His shrill and unearthly voice sends a chill up her spine, but she manages to keep calm as she takes a seat.

"My name is Dr... Rizwan," she replies. "I know exactly where I am."

"Of course you are. That white coat wouldn't be much of a disguise if you weren't."

He turns his body toward her, though still sitting in the lotus position. This sudden movement does make her shift her position a bit in her chair.

"Let me guess, are you also here to talk to me? To ask me those same stupid questions they've all asked for all these years? Do you think *you'll* get different answers from me?"

"All I want is the truth."

"Heh," he grunts. "They all said the same thing too. Rizwan. Unusual name for a girl."

"It's my father's name."

"Ah, I see," he smirks behind the veil of his hair. "Wouldn't want me to know more about you, would you?"

"What makes you think I'm afraid of telling you my first name?"

"Because if you knew anything about me, if they told you anything about me before you came here; you would know that the more knowledge I have of you, the easier it becomes for me to bend you to my will."

"Ah yes, the whole magician routine." She chuckles.

"Magician?" He grunts as he finally begins to rise.

And as he does so, the Doctor gets a good look at his body riddled with injuries and tattoos of all kinds, some of them darker and more sinister in nature than she has ever seen before.

"Do you smell that?" He asks, sniffing something in the air. "It's you, you have the whiff of something oddly familiar."

She grimaces a little and shakes her head.

"It's mosquito repellant. Jasmine flavored."

"Fancy," he snickers.

"Does that help you with your silly magician routine?"

"I don't do magic, girl!" he declares as he gets closer to the bars. "I am a sorcerer of the dark arts, a *jaadugarr*."

"Yes, I believe that's what you've told my predecessors. Though isn't it just a cover for all kinds of crimes? Hypnotism, terror, murders and the acts of cannibalism you perpetrated or had perpetrated by other hapless people are just some of the acts of violence that come under your notions of 'jaadugarri.'"

"You mock me, child."

"It's *Doctor!*" She rebukes sternly.

"Of course, I meant no disrespect. Certainly not like when you called me a magician."

"Interesting how you're able to speak English fluently, and yet you're unable to discern how both those words are just translations."

"You say that because you have no inkling of what they both are," he continues to chuckle. "Magicians are just simple charlatans who entertain children at birthday parties. My craft is a lot more than some overdressed entertainer's plain act of pulling a rabbit out of a hat."

"Oh I don't deny that. The trail of bodies you have left behind attest to your gruesome occupation. But it's all just a scam. Convincing people that killing their relatives and drinking their blood would give them unlimited power or eternal youth, putting them under mind control to make them commit violent crimes of all kind, having them cannibalize their victims just to remove the evidence... As a criminal psychologist, it all makes for one heck of a research study."

"But you've yet to touch upon my crowning achievement. The reason why I am who I am, why all of you keep me down here. Surely they told you that already."

The Doctor raises an eyebrow, not exactly confirming whether what he said was true or not.

"Why don't you enlighten me?"

"The *Jinn*," he snickers.

"Excuse me?"

"It was the oddest thing, really. Before he came into my life, I was exactly what you said I was. Did exactly what you said I did. I didn't stop, of course. Only intensified all of it just so I could get his power."

"Whose power?" She asks. "This jinn's?"

"Funny how life can deal you a cruel twist of fate. This jinn came to our world, to this very country and became part of humanity. Though he didn't come by choice, he came because, you'll find this very amusing ... glasses."

"Come again?"

The prisoner looks underneath his chin and his hand grabs something from behind his beard. Apparently he was also wearing something around his neck on a thread. His hand brings it forward and Dr. Rizwan sees two pieces of a pair of steel-framed goggles, broken at the center and the lenses inside completely shattered. Seeing this, her brow tightens as she leans a bit forward.

"His vision had deteriorated, you see, and his masters had sent him down to our world so he could get prescription glasses. For some reason, he decided to make a vacation out of it and started living with a family of humans. He had an affinity for some children and befriended them. I discovered the fool frolicking with them, completely oblivious to what I had in store for him. His power is what I had wanted, power that would make me the sole master of this world."

"Power of a jinn? Do you actually believe that?"

"You seem like a woman of faith. Don't you believe in their existence?"

"That's beside the point," she replies. "Jinns don't just play with children."

"Whatever you choose to believe is up to you," he brings the glasses back to their hanging position around his neck. "But I made it my life's purpose to gain his powers, to take all he had and turn it against the world. And in doing so, I sacrificed a great deal. They took my sister."

"Your partner in your schemes?" She opens the file resting on her lap and flips a few pages. "Our records show she disappeared when you did in the mid-90s and was never seen again. What did you do to her?"

The prisoner looks back at her, his eyes burning with rage as he bangs the bars of the cell.

"She was my sister!" He screams. "I would never harm her. It was that horned half-wit, the other jinn who banded together with the first jinn."

"Another jinn?" She smirks, rolling her eyes. "Right, of course. Because one jinn isn't enough for you."

"This one was just a mere half-wit, only interested in looking for his next task and meal. But the one with the glasses was my ticket to unlimited power. And so when they thought they had destroyed me, they returned back to their kingdom and left the world of humans forever. What they didn't know at the time is that I had not been destroyed."

"Then?"

"My essence had merely been scattered around the cosmos. I wandered aimlessly throughout all of space and time, but my hatred for those two gave me purpose. Throughout that time, I garnered powers and abilities, other forms of *jaadu* that had been unknown to me. Dark arts from lost civilizations, forbidden witchcraft that had destroyed worlds and shattered existence time and again. Abilities that allowed me to return to Earth to seek my revenge. I even picked up a sense of telepathy, which is why I can extract the knowledge of the English language from your mind.

Dr. Rizwan cocks her head and smirks again.

"Really, so you can talk to me in English because you learned it from my mind."

"A minor trifle, really. Skills are easily gained because you use them automatically. Different from your memories because you hold them much closer to your being. But all of the jaadu I had acquired would be incomplete till my rage had been satiated. Till I had achieved what I truly desired. So I returned to Earth, and unleashed havoc. A reign of terror across the land that shone like a beacon to the kingdom of Jinns."

He put his hands on the bar and began to laugh, salivating along the way.

"The horned half-wit was the first to come. He thought he could face me and vanquish me again like before. All on his own, the imbecile! But he had grown weak and feeble doing nothing all the time since he had left this world. I was the only one who truly brought out the best in him. He was the first I took down, and I added his pitiful power to my own. His death was just to bring *him* back to me."

"The jinn with spectacles?" She pondered.

"He thought he could reason with me. Thought he could make me see the error of my ways. Believed he could make me use my powers for good. He was a fool as always. He trembled in front of all the power I had, but *his* was truly what would make it all complete for me. At this point it wasn't about who was more powerful. It was about what I was owed. All the pain and suffering, all the humiliation and sacrifice I endured because of him had to be settled. So we waged battle, fought tooth and nail, his powers against mine. But in the end, his compassion for all living things made him weak, whereas my rage was supreme. And once I was about to deliver the killing blow, he tried one last gambit to escape by trying to discorporate himself and return to his home. But I harnessed his essence, absorbed all his power, and it remains inside me to this day. All that power, all that energy from the entire universe fuelling the power of the Jinn, and vice versa! It made me master of all I surveyed."

Grabbing the bars, the sound of steel bending in his hands startles Dr. Rizwan who almost sits up. The prisoner looks back at her and laughs again.

"You fear me. It's not your fault. It's only natural."

He takes his hands off the bars and gestures her to relax.

"So you took his power, became master of all you surveyed," Dr. Rizwan keeps a sense of her bluster. "Tell me, what kind of master sits inside a cage?"

"Ah," he grins. "Now there's a question they've never asked before. You are astute if nothing else."

"It's fairly straightforward. You claim to have so much power and yet you don't seem to be sitting on some dark throne having everyone do your bidding."

"What makes you think I'm not?" He retorts. "Look around you. Your world lives on the whims of evil and humanity is consumed by hatred and rage. Your incidents of terrorism and the wars that subsequently followed them, your culture of bigotry and violence for people of different faiths and skins, your unquenchable desire to kill over mere baubles and trinkets of this modern age. And worst of all, the evil that doesn't even spare children from its ungodly wrath."

"You're saying *you've* caused all this?"

"I remember it as clear as day when this century began. The flying machines that killed so many in those buildings. The fear, the panic, the burning desire of vengeance that was born of it. And that continued to fester within humanity, making everyday trivialities fuel the darkness inside all of them. A violent husband, a misguided bully, the cruel taunts of a heartless mistress, the backbreaking demands of the modern slave masters, the unflinching eyes of the torturer looking for information from prisoners, the insatiable and unholy lust of the monsters that doesn't distinguish between size, age or gender. All of it was a result of unleashing the blight on to this world, a blight that hovers over everyone like a dark cloud that threatens to bring about the worst in anyone the minute they step on someone else's shoes."

"That's just ridiculous."

"You think?" The prisoner spits on the floor. "Then tell me, good doctor. Do you have children?"

"No." She replies. "Not my own, anyways."

"Then you must know exactly what I mean. Tell me how many times you've held them close, how you've reprimanded them every time they escape your sight in the middle of a crowd. How you've held them close while a pair of eyes so much as stares at them. That is, unless you're warding off the eyes from yourself."

"Not everyone is a monster."

"Perhaps. But that doesn't mean there aren't any among us. Back when you were a child, your parents must have let you have the run of the town. Even those children associated with the jinn and thwarted my plans felt safer in their times."

"And you say you've created this evil among people."

"Who knows. Perhaps the evil was already there. I've just brought out humanity's true nature. And for that, I am master of all and prisoner of none. I will be the king when this world turns into something even hell would blush against. And once all is under my power, every man, woman and child will worship me."

"While you're still inside this prison?" Dr. Rizwan smirks.

"This is merely a refuge till I need to rise. Till the day I foresee will come, and come soon. The *jaadu* will keep me alive for untold centuries yet, and till then, this is as good a place as any to remain."

"Right, *that's* the reason. You know, instead of the one where they caught you for your crimes and put you down in this deep cellar so you wouldn't be among humanity ever again."

"Those rags in the corner were meant to subdue me, but they were not enough," the prisoner then raises his arms to show her the broken metal bands. "They tried to shackle me, chain me. I could leave this place anytime I want, but I choose not to. I wait for the day when it is time for me to rise."

"Fascinating! Truly fascinating!" The Doctor gets up from her chair and closes her file. "Your entire story is so well crafted and absolutely visceral. The way you believe in it will be cause for greater breakthroughs in the psychology field."

"You still think this is a fantasy," the prisoner's voice is stern now, still retaining its shrill quality. "Despite what I've told you, your mind cannot accept it."

"I accept facts. And the simple fact is you're nothing but an evil man who did evil things to innocents. And whatever evil plagues this world is a consequence of humanity's own choices. Certainly nothing to do with whatever black power you're so proud of."

"I don't believe it."

"Believe what?"

"In all these years I've been here, none have accomplished what you have."

Just then, the shackles on the prisoner's hands glow red as they finally break off his wrists. His forearms begin to burn in a kind of black fire that glistens around him now.

"You've managed to goad me into showing you my true power. You wanted to have a demonstration of what I can do. Very well, you will see first-hand that I am no *pantaloons jaadugarr!*"

"What did you say?" Dr. Rizwan gasps as she moves forward toward the cage.

"You will bear witness..." the prisoners eyes glow red as the power begins to course inside his body, his voice beginning to echo inside the chamber, "... to the dark powers at my command, as I destroy everyone in this entire building. Sadly for you, it will be the last thing you ever see."

But as soon as he says it, his voice chokes and he grabs his throat with both his hands. He feels pain unlike anything he has ever felt before, like something being pulled out from inside him. It's only when he looks outside that he sees Dr. Rizwan standing firm, holding aloft an open silver locket on a chain. To his horror, swirls of black smoke escape from his body and make their way inside the locket till nothing else remains inside him. The Doctor then closes the locket shut and puts it back around her neck.

"No, *that* locket!" the prisoner now falls to his knees, weak as he holds on to the bars for support. "I *know* that locket. Where did you get it? Tell me!"

"It belonged to my brother. It was given to him by a jinn. A jinn with spectacles."

"No!" A sense of realization appears on the prisoner's face. "The boy! The children. You have his scent. You're his sister. You're the *girl.*"

The Doctor steps much closer to the bars, now that the prisoner can barely move.

"My name... is *Moattar.*"

On hearing this, the prisoner gasps as he falls flat on the floor, his skin beginning to constrict around his skeletal frame.

"Of course. I should have come for you. You two always managed to help that jinn foil my plans. I... I should have realized..."

"That's right. You should have," Moattar looks down at him with the same stone-faced expression. "But you took our friend from us, from his family."

She then touches the locket once, and it shimmers with a white light.

"I'm just making sure he returns home."

"Where will you take him?" He manages to ask.

"They're waiting for him to return to *Qafqaz.* It has been a long wait. And you? You can continue to rule your kingdom of the basement cell."

Dr. Moattar turns around and picks up her file from the chair to head for the stairs.

"You think you've won," a barely audible cackle makes her stop and turn around.

"No, you've lost. For good, this time."

"No, I haven't. I've accomplished what I wanted to. I have turned this world into the epitome of darkness and evil it was meant to be. Even if I can't rule it, I'll die content in the knowledge that there won't be much left of it soon."

"Whatever powers you used to turn this world to the way it is have left you now," Moattar replies as she takes a few steps into the light. "It will restore humanity to the way it was, and rid it of evil. Maybe not overnight, maybe it'll take years. But there is goodness enough in people to come out of this blight you created."

"Believe all you like," the prisoner now shakes and trembles as he keeps lying flat on his back, his body getting weaker by the second. "Your world is doomed."

Moattar steps closer to the cell and looks down at the now dying prisoner.

"Goodbye... *Hamuun.*"

She finally turns around and climbs up the stairs. The light bulb switches off as the door shuts for good, with the moonlight shining over a decayed corpse surrounded by pantaloons.

RAPTURE

The elevator door dings open and Sabreena strolls out, the carpet-lined corridor doing its best to suppress the sound of her stiletto heels attempting to make their familiar clacking sound. Her small satchel rests steadily over her waist as her white t-shirt, and a caramel colored jacket and pair of black jeans cling to her slim frame. Her hair, though appears to be straight and flowing, is a result of a few hours with a hair straightener to bring them out of their wavy and curly shape.

As she walks down the corridor looking left and right, her heart begins to beat faster and her throat begins to well up with anxiety. It has been quite some time since her last client and certainly a very long one since she was hired for a complete package. While the flesh trade pays great dividends in the short term, the long term career prospects of staying in it are sparse. Even though she's done her best to stay relatively appealing, there is an endless supply of call girls who ply their trade all over the world. And in a city like hers, age is an unforgiving inevitability.

Years ago, she lived a calm and comfortable life with the money she was getting as a high-paid escort and had a diverse client base for which she would do anything and everything. But as the years wore on, her clients dried up faster than the moisture in her cheeks. Her body, long ravaged and used and abused by the whims of lust had lost the sheen that made her skin so tempting to touch. Her eyes had seen far too much and witnessed acts on herself that remain forever etched in her irises, making them lose their gleam whenever her clients looked into them.

That's not something they wanted to see, she discovered. They didn't want to see their reflections through mirrors of agony. Certainly not from the toys they were paying good money for. How could they manage an erection if all they had in front of them were damaged goods?

Finally stopping at her destination, the label of Room 515 stares Sabreena right in the eyes as she takes stock of herself. She straightens her dress and runs a few fingers through her hair to give herself a boost of confidence, takes a deep breath and knocks. Even after all of these years, she remembers how to keep her composure for the task ahead. And considering she had been hired for delivering the complete package, Sabreena had to make sure she was well prepared both physically and mentally for the night. It was indeed going to be a long one after what feels like ages.

"Come in. It's not locked."

She opens the door and passes through the foyer of the small, dimly-lit room to find him lying down on the couch next to the bed. Wearing a silken black robe with his bare legs sticking out and resting on the armrests, she can only assume he isn't exactly a strapping tall, young and handsome man one encounters in the erotica movies, but more middle-aged and physically portly with relatively good height. Which isn't exactly a problem for Sabreena, as in her line of work such customers are plentiful considering they need an escape from their own mundane existences. Married men, divorcees, separated, businessmen and even bureaucrats who simply don't have the time or energy to cope with the rigors of married life are just some of these people who prefer hiring escorts to satiate their desires.

And sometimes there are the strange ones like him who have a certain rule escorts are supposed to abide by depending on the fee. And as she looks at his bearded face and the cowl wrapped around his head and the area above his nose with just two openings for the eyes, Sabreena remembers the specific instructions she was given about ensuring the man's identity would remain a secret. Meaning Sabreena would have to curb her own relative curiosity and definitely not try to peek behind the mask, which shouldn't be a problem considering the significant amount of money she was being paid.

"Please, sit down and make yourself comfortable."

With the sole two-seater being occupied by the man, Sabreena makes her way towards the bed and sits down in front of him crossing her legs and laying her handbag next to her. She begins to radiate a smile she has done so many times over so many years to make sure her clients get their money's worth.

"Very nice to meet you in person," she says, smiling.

"You took the words right out of my mouth," he replies as he sits upright and leans towards her to get a better look, which also allows Sabreena to do the same.

"So," she continues, "you certainly are a man of mystery. I don't think I've ever had the pleasure of meeting you before. And my contacts don't know much about you either."

"You're disappointed?"

"Not at all." She continues to smile. "It's just that we tend to be more at ease with people we're familiar with so that way we know what to expect. And well, you are coming to us for the first time..."

"Oh, I'm sorry," he sounds sincere. "I should have realized you would have your reasons to be apprehensive about absolute strangers, even if your contacts had any idea about them. Plus, I'm sure the mask doesn't help either."

She smirks, beginning to regain her level of comfort.

"Yes, there is that. But then, I guess you're paying a good deal of money to make sure I don't poke my nose where it's not wanted. Um, speaking of which, I'm sure you were told we prefer to be paid up front."

"Ah yes, of course. Where are my manners? Top drawer."

Sabreena leans towards the bedside table and pulls out a small bag from the drawer. Unzipping it, she stares wide-eyed at the pack of US Dollars inside.

"I assure you," he mentions, "it's all there. But please, feel free to make sure. And do keep the bag."

She thumbs through a few of the dollar bills inside before she zips the bag up and puts it on the bedside table, while also leaving her own handbag next to it.

"This is more than generous of you," she states.

"Absolutely not. If it meant meeting you, I would pay more than this."

"That's um, another thing that puzzled me," Sabreena says, running her forefinger over a stray strand of hair. "Hope you don't mind if I ask, but you requested for *me* specifically. I'm sure you must have seen the catalog but you picked me out of so many others. It's as if you knew about me."

"If you mean that I was told about you by one of your clients, then no. Well, since you've brought it up, I should mention I'm actually a huge fan of yours, from back in the day when you were on TV."

Hearing this, Sabreena's radiant smile begins to falter as he opens the floodgates to so many memories of a bygone era. Of another lifetime she had tried her hardest to forget, or at least bury in the deepest pits of her mind. And with just a single, casual compliment by him, it all comes rushing out like a volcanic eruption.

"Oh," she exclaims, "you know about the uh..."

"Is that a problem?" He wonders. "I thought you would be flattered."

"No it's just," she hesitates as she looks for the right words, "it's just something I haven't thought of in a long time."

"Yes, I wondered why you disappeared from the screens. You were so wonderful back in the day and had many in your thrall. Case in point."

She smirks as he gestures to himself.

"Well, I don't really think about it that much anymore. Things just have a way of not working out the way you want them to. I guess you could chalk this up to an experience that opened my eyes."

"Do you want to tell me about it?"

Sabreena looks at him with a raised eyebrow.

"You're not a reporter or something, are you?"

"Do I look like a reporter?" He replies, nonchalantly.

"No, I guess you're not. But you are asking a lot of questions."

"I was told as part of the complete package, I could do as I pleased."

At the mention of this, Sabreena does lower her eyes as she feels as if she has made a mistake. One that might cost her greatly.

"But it's alright," he continues as he gets up from the couch. "I suppose it wasn't what you were expecting at all, so I may have come off strong there."

"No, it's not that," she tries to salvage the night. "I uh..."

"Shhh, it's okay. Besides..."

He unstraps his gown and it falls off of his body, revealing his chubby but glistening frame covered only in a pair of boxer shorts.

"We do have all night."

He reaches out to her hand and picks her up as they hold each other in a soft embrace. Feeling the warmth between the two, Sabreena welcomes his lips to hers as they enter a passionate kiss. She lets him take her in his hands as she relishes in his soft and delicate touch, while not objecting as he begins to relieve her of her upper garments. Welcoming his gentle caresses, she makes her way to the bed as he begins to get his money's worth. But Sabreena could feel it meant something more to him. It was as if he had waited for this for a very long time, and now he was finally quenching his thirst as his hands and lips took in her delicate body.

Even for Sabreena, who had been out of the game for quite a while, who had been deprived of her regular business as she took a beating from the ravages of time, the sensations of a man finally deriving pleasure from her was akin to having a whiff of a narcotic she had long forgotten. That and the fact he and his money had come to her after having been mercilessly shunned by her loyal clientele put her mind at ease, which made it easier for her body to be far more accommodating to his whims.

The experience itself is nothing new to Sabreena, but she is a bit amazed at the level of delicateness and passion the man treats her with. Having been with all sorts in her lifetime, she knows of all kinds of manners in which men treat their merchandise. Some like to be gentle, some prefer to be rough. There are even the sadists who take pleasure in being violent and causing a bit of harm to their playthings, but she has to endure a certain limit so long as the money outweighs any concerns. But with him, it feels as if there is something more genuine to the way he treats her. The care and tenderness he exhibits almost make her feel as if he considers her more than just merchandise. That it all comes from a deep place in his heart.

And so does the pain, as his gentle touches turn a bit rough when he grabs her all over. His passion becomes excessive as he now begins to ravish her more harshly with his kisses, now utilizing his teeth more than his lips. But even as his tender warmth turns more hostile and searing, even as his grip turns more punishing than caring, Sabreena does not object for she feels it all comes from a place of love in him. That this excessiveness, this harshness, this animalistic desire stems from a deep-rooted feeling of ardor he must have for her. That all he can now focus on is to make her completely his as he tears at her with his fingers and nails, marking her as his and his alone and taking over her completely.

And so she reciprocates his animalistic urges, pulls him closer onto her and returns his thrusts with her own. She delves into his desires with her gasps and moans of delight just to let him know she is indeed now entirely his.

*

"I always wanted to be a star," she finally says, catching her breath next to him as they both are spent from their passionate revels.

"Is that a fact?"

"I didn't come from a well-off background," she continues. "I didn't have any family in the industry and I never knew how to navigate through the murky world behind showbiz. It may look so shiny and glamorous from the outside, but inside it was just too ugly to become a part of. Everyone who wanted to be successful in it had to pay their dues, and with the amount of private TV channels that began to mushroom across the country, the standards of management began to get far too low."

"Oh yes, I heard." He rests upright on his pillow with his head resting on his hands. "They would rather cast someone who would get into bed with them than on their own acting merits."

Sabreena looks at him with her eyes trying to fight some tears, showing them in an innocent light. She pulls herself towards him and rests her head on his abdomen.

"It was my choice, I know. I just wanted it so bad that I didn't know better. I ran away from school just to get into it all, but the more I got into it, the more I discovered I needed to pay a toll for every time I would be on screen. And so I did."

"Must have been hard on your family."

"Oh the acting gig wasn't exactly a very lucrative one, considering there were many more like me willing to shed their dignity for the spotlight. But it did get me into the escort business. Apparently one thing inevitably led to the other and I just couldn't find my way out of it. And of course, the money was very good. Very, *very* good in fact. I paid for my sister to get through a good college and she... well she's *acting* too nowadays."

"Oh?"

"Yeah, I guess she realized there was more money to be made. But she's making quite a lot to save for a foreign university. Kids these days are just too idealistic."

"Do you regret it?" He asks, gently caressing her hair. "Missing out on your education I mean?"

"Not really. I don't regret anything. Hell, I even got language and elocution lessons from the money I made so I could be more *cosmopolitan*."

"That's a great way to invest in yourself."

"I made my choice and my peace with it all. You can't change how the world works, you know. There's always a price to pay."

"What about love?"

This question does take her by surprise.

"Love?" She looks up at him. "What about it?"

"Come on!" He says, caressing her hair. "You can't really tell me you've never had feelings for anyone. Or that anyone hasn't loved you for just *you* rather than your body."

"No one's ever asked me that before," Sabreena appears to be genuinely flummoxed.

"It's a simple enough question. Perhaps you've asked it of yourself."

Sabreena continues to look at him, his face still obscured by the cowl but his eyes still able to show his honesty.

"Can't say I have." She answers, taking a deep breath.

"So you're telling me there's been no one in your life who you could see a future with? No one at all?"

Sabreena chuckles as she considers the thought. A memory returns to her, one that had never occurred to her lately much like her time as an actress till he brought it up.

"No, not at all. And even if there was anyone... it wouldn't have worked."

"Why not?"

"Because..." she looks away, a nervous smile on her face, "... look at me. I'm not the sort of woman who would want to just settle down. I'm in this far too deep to get out of it now, and I don't think some hapless love-stricken fool would be able to keep me accustomed to the lifestyle I was used to."

"Is that what you tell yourself? That you're just too high-maintenance?"

"As opposed to what?" She wonders, biting her lip.

"The truth. That you wouldn't want to be unfair to someone who loved you so much by being what you are."

Sabreena looks away from him and does ponder at what he says, smiling just a bit yet again.

"You are amazing, you know," she says. "You truly see the best in people, even someone like me."

He smiles back at her.

"Are you happy though? With what you do, with how it all turned out?"

"I guess. Though lately I wouldn't know since I haven't been doing it much."

"You quit?" He asks, raising an eyebrow.

"Ha, I wish!" She laughs. "Before you came along, I was actually kind of desperate for a client. My own savings were running out and well, I haven't been cast in anything ever since I took up escorting full-time. I moved from Karachi to Dubai just because of the money, but without clients these days it's becoming tougher. I do work at a mall for a day job, but it isn't as glamorous or well-paying as this. You're my first in a long while, and your generosity is out of this world."

"Has it been that bad?"

"Hehe, like the acting world, age is our biggest flaw. Time doesn't wait for anyone, and once you begin to lose your luster, the world doesn't notice you. Hence my surprise when you found me in the catalog. I couldn't believe it when my contact told me you picked me out specifically despite his recommendations for other fresher ones."

"I told you, I wanted you more than anything."

His hand gently strokes her back as it makes its way under the covers and over her naked flesh, arousing her yet again as she slowly makes her way up to face him right into his eyes, his face still wrapped in the cowl.

"And the night is still young."

So they begin once more, the same dance over and over multiple times. He as the caring and affectionate lover at first, then turning more bestial and dominating as it progresses. She as the forest of plenty craving this reaping of her fruit and welcoming his warmth and viciousness, unable to help herself as rapture overcomes her very being. She can't help but wonder if the money she's getting is just secondary compared to the absolute pleasure both of them are experiencing. Her mind continues to erupt in the pleasurable sensations her body is communicating to it, as it tries to decipher the mystery behind her generous benefactor. The man who has seemingly changed her life overnight with every ounce of love and lust he sends her way.

She looks for answers in his eyes as she mounts him, peering deep behind the curtain of the cowl to find a glimmer of anything that would satiate her curiosity. But all she could find in his eyes was his raging desire for her, which did tell her there was something primal in him that would take all from her that she had, ravage her body and soul completely. And he does this all in his love for her. Love that she cannot fathom to even exist. Love that is unquestioning, passionate, and violent to rock her being. It is love, that much she knows. And for some reason, it is one that is oddly familiarizing itself to her in a way no other man had ever done.

*

She couldn't sleep. Not after all that had transpired. Not even after the man had succumbed to slumber on his side of the bed in the early hours of the morning. Her mind races to process all the sensations she had experienced, reliving everything over and over again wishing for it to never end. But as the early glints of dawn began to pierce through from beneath the curtains of the room, she knew this engagement had ended, and the transaction had been completed.

With a twinge of regret, she heads for the shower but even the water isn't able to quench her thirst for pleasure as well as answers. She finds her clothes to get dressed and collects her satchel. Looking at the money in the small bag one last time, she zips it up and is about to leave when she stops in her tracks to look back at him.

"Just one peek. He won't know."

She carefully approaches him with his head resting comfortably on the pillow and his cowl having become loose over the night. She had perhaps subconsciously tried to rip it away from his face while in the throes of her passion, and he had managed to keep it intact over his head. Nevertheless, all it would take was a gentle pull for her to discover just who it was under the hood.

And when she did, when the briefest layer of sunlight showed her his face, Sabreena was at first unmoved simply because she couldn't quite place him right away. Certainly no one she had met before in her line of work. And even if she had, the beard made him completely unrecognizable. But her mind began to peel back the layers slowly, began to erase the facial hair and the wrinkles of age and the scars of time the face had endured, till at last the familiarity began to engulf her mind.

Her memories began to rush out over the different topics of conversation they had. Of a friend she had all those years ago from her time as an actress who was inseparable from her. Of a boy who she had continued to text every night after her tiring late-night endeavors as an escort. Of someone who was her escape from the brutal toil her nights as a call girl had taken on her. Or not an escape, but her tether to a saner world. Of a man she found herself needing to stay pure and innocent of the unforgiving world she lived in, and to remain oblivious of her life so she could have something even close to normal.

And of course, of the one who had ruined it all just by declaring his love for her. That is what Sabreena could not stand, that is what she hated the most: a misguided love-stricken fool who thought they could be together forever.

So she abandoned him without a second thought, smothered her ringing phone under a pillow, blocked his number from ever calling her again and cut off all ties with him. And thus she relegated him to a memory forever lost in the deep recesses of her mind.

Till now.

As the realization hits her, Sabreena drops the cowl on the floor and takes a few steps back. She can't believe it is him after all this time, after all these years. She can't believe she even remembers him, but even behind the beard and the wrinkles on his face, she can remember his eyes now with the same passion of last night as it was all those years ago. With a love that was actually so genuine that she had never even considered being possible.

And in the course of a single night, he had given her all he had ever felt for her. His unquestioning love, his unbridled passion, his pure and primal lust... all that had been simmering within him, reaching fever pitch and finally exploding last night. Years of love, years of longing; all of it finally making its way to her in the most unlikeliest of events. And it is a message she has received both body and soul, and it has left her completely separated from her sense of reality.

She can only stand shocked beyond belief, the torrent of memories and emotions hitting her like a hurricane against a mountain. A mountain that is doing all within its power not to crumble. Clutching her bag of money, she turns around to leave when his voice stops her dead in her tracks.

"If you had told me then of who you were, of what you did... I'm sure I could have paid you."

Sabreena turns around, tears now flowing down her cheeks from her eyes as they stare back at him. She had been hearing his voice all night, and had failed to place it with the sweet, innocent voice of her friend from yesteryear. It now sounded more weathered, more pained and one that had waited to speak to her for eons. And unlike last night, when his voice sounded warmer and more caring, it now seemed to shoot daggers at her.

"I mean, I don't know if I could have afforded a night with you at the time, but maybe you might have given me a friend's discount?"

"You... you knew?" She manages to ask as her voice begins to choke, her throat dry and her mouth parched.

"They told me," he sits upright, taking a deep breath as he relives a past only he had experienced and she had never considered. "They all told me, warned me about you and your actual *profession*. But I didn't believe it. I was too blinded by you, not just your beauty but by your friendliness. You were just too caring a person for me to think the worst of you. The way you would text me at odd hours, the way you would devote your time to me, always going out of the way to be my friend. I almost thought I couldn't cope with you. I knew one day I would slip up and disappoint you so much that you would never want to talk to me again. But that never happened. You never saw the worst in me."

The tears begin to flood out of her face, as she can no longer hold back her emotions and begins crying. But he doesn't stop.

"Until you stopped picking up my calls of course. Until you left me all by myself, shattered and in a mess with no one there to console me and understand what I was going through. The only one who could have was you. But then I had to know. I needed to have my answers. So I called them, people who had told me about you. Got help from them and so I followed you to the hotels with one person or the other, sometimes more than one. Till I dressed up like a member of staff and brought room service to your room, with all the clothes strewn on the floor and you on the bed and your knees. With them."

"What?" She appears genuinely shocked as the tears show no sign of ceasing. "When did you..."

"Does it matter?"

"But, why?" She barely manages to ask. "Why did you do all of this, now after all these years?"

"To prove you right of course," he chuckles. "To justify the real reason you left me. Because to you, I was just another man who wanted nothing more from you than a pound of flesh. Because you knew my whole lovesick façade was just a way to get into your pants. Just like everyone else."

"No, I never thought that of you!" She cries. "You're right, you were special to me. Someone who was put in my life just to be something for me. Someone who wasn't what I would share for money. Someone who cared, who just stayed with me for me. You were always my best friend. The best one I ever had."

"Yeah," he sighs as his shoulders slope down. "Too bad it was never enough for you. You probably never even gave me a second thought after you ended it all."

He gets up from the bed and finds his boxers from the floor.

"Take the money and go. Live your life. Be happy."

She looks back at him one last time, the tears still glistening in her eyes.

"Will I... will I ever see you again?" she asks, trying to put up a weak smile as her heart undergoes a torrent of emotional turmoil. "Is there going to be another moment for us?"

He looks at her expressionless, trying his best to hold back his tears and from tearing up the walls that keep his own emotions - his own true feelings - at bay. He walks up to her slowly and holds her face in his hands.

"Oh Sabreena, there is no *us*. You made sure of that all those years ago."

With those words, he makes his way to the bathroom without even looking back at her for an instant. The sound of the shower drowns out the sound of her sobbing. Wiping her tears away, hoping for something more to happen, Sabreena at last takes the money and walks out of the room, her steps barely able to sustain the weight of her aching heart.

<u>05</u>

CHOICES

"That's it, turn left, you're almost there."

Qudsia frantically puts the tray of cookies in the oven while nestling her smartphone between her shoulder and ear, taking care not to drop any cookies from the tray or the entire order would be ruined. Once the timer has been set, she returns to the flour batter she's been mixing and continues to give directions over the phone.

"Yeah, I know exactly where I'm sending you. I send orders there all the time. You'll see a huge park on your right, and the gate is a few buildings ahead. Yeah, once you're at the gate, turn around and come to the second building. Yeah, that's right, turn around at the gate and stop at the second building."

This is an ordinary Tuesday for Qudsia. Domestic bliss may have felt good after getting married, however she wasn't built for lounging about at home. All through her life, she had honed her skills at baking delicious desserts and treats, so it stands to reason she would occupy her time in sharing the fruit of her talents with everyone else. And with the advent of social media enabling anyone and everyone to conduct business on the Internet equipped with nothing more than a smartphone and a dedicated data plan, Qudsia quickly established herself as a premium online bakery with a burgeoning and loyal customer base.

"Because if you stop from across the building, you'll likely be a victim of the speeding motorcycles on the street. And if anything happens to that three-tier cake... Glad you see my point. Later."

Disconnecting the call, she continues working on her next order while making sure she has enough time for the cookies to get ready. Checking her delivery app to ensure the customer to whom she sent the rider to has confirmed receipt of the order, she sighs in relief as she sees the five-star rating getting updated on her service ID. Right after the ding of her phone, the sound of the doorbell echoes through the house catching Qudsia's attention.

"Uh oh."

Checking the timer on the oven once more, she heads to the front door of her apartment.

"Yes?" she asks on the door intercom.

"Hello, my name is Ms. Ghazal. We have an appointment."

"Oh, right. Yes!"

Opening the door, Qudsia welcomes the older woman appearing to be in her mid-forties, dressed in rather upscale branded clothes. Qudsia notices the woman likes to look young judging from her fashionably elegant choice in hairstyle and make-up. As she offers her a place on the living room sofa, Qudsia is about to sit herself when she remembers something.

"Oh shoot, just a moment."

She heads back into the kitchen while Ms. Ghazal looks around the living room and smiles with a deep breath. Qudsia returns with a tray of one-bite samosas.

"I hope you like them. They're not very fattening."

"Oh dear, you shouldn't have!" Ghazal remarks, while picking one from the tray as Qudsia sets it on the table.

"Just trying a new recipe. I'm about to introduce it on my menu."

"Yes, you seem to have your hands full. Some of your customers are good friends of mine, and they simply adore your items. It's how I got to know you needed help with your... uh..."

"My daughter, yes. She's four and has been going to school for a year now. And while I thought it would work out somehow with my baking business, I guess I didn't expect to get this successful, with Allah's grace."

"Indeed. A friend of mine showed me your post where you mentioned you need a governess."

"Is that what I need?" Qudsia chuckles. "I was just out looking for a nanny."

"They're both the same thing." Ghazal grins. "But of course you've got to brand yourself a certain way. Besides, imagine telling your friends you've got a governess. And before you know it, everyone will start calling for one."

"Sounds a bit snobbish, no offence."

"None taken, dear. But that's not the only reason why I call myself one. See back in the day, a governess was with the child all the time and entrusted to take care of upbringing, education; with the parents' approval of course. Nowadays, the Saudi royal families are also employing governesses as well."

"That makes sense, but my daughter does go to school. So I'm sure the set curriculum is the way to go."

"Oh don't worry about these things, those are just trivial matters. And like I said, *you* would be my boss."

"I hope you don't mind if I ask," Qudsia carefully broaches the subject, "but you don't seem like the governess type. I mean, you do look more, uh..."

"Rich?"

"I'd say cultured."

"Well yes, I am both those things. But much like you, we do have to occupy the time. Plus I'm sure you became a baker because you were good at it. Same is the case with me and taking care of children. I've had years of experience taking care of my siblings' children and when word passed around, I began my own day care. A lot of very wealthy people came to me and entrusted me with their children. I have kept up certain standards."

"Yeah, I did look you up."

"Did you?" Ghazal inquires.

"Yeah, I was very impressed. Actually, more than that: overwhelmed. From what you've done with child upbringing and your work with different homes for orphans and underprivileged kids..."

"Oh, you know quite a lot, dear!"

"It wasn't hard to ignore."

"And good on your part to do your due diligence. That's very responsible parenting."

"Well, this is my daughter we're talking about. So you can imagine I'm being a bit apprehensive about why someone like you - someone of your scope I mean - would want to come to me in this apartment and take care of my daughter. I mean, surely your own daycare thing should be occupying your attention."

"Oh I don't take care of it anymore. I am the figurehead founder of course, but my nieces take care of all that these days. They've proven themselves to be quite adept at running things now. They have been for a few years, which allowed me to get into doing consultancy work for different organizations. You know, schools, child development and welfare organizations; no rest for the weary I'm afraid."

"That sounds... overwhelming like I said," Qudsia chuckles again. "I mean, apart from everything else, I wouldn't even know what to pay you."

"Oh dear, is that what's concerning you?" Ghazal guffaws. "You don't need to, really. I'm just trying to keep myself in the game, so I'm looking to get back to my roots as it were. And this would be a perfect new start."

"Also, I wanted to ask you this, but every question I've asked so far includes the words *I hope you don't mind* in it, so..."

"Oh but of course dear," Ghazal sounds genuinely warm, while gulping another samosa, "please don't hold back. It's your child's welfare you're concerned about, and I'm practically a stranger to you."

"Well, with everything you've done and everything you've accomplished, it just occurred to me how you never actually had children of your own."

"Oh... uhhh..."

At this question, Ghazal does seem to lose her stride a bit and appears slightly protective of herself. Lucky for her though, the oven timer dings loud enough to catch Qudsia's attention.

"Oh shoot, just a second," Qudsia exclaims as she hops off her sofa, "I really need to attend to this batch. Would you care for some tea? I'll put the kettle on."

"Oh uh, sure dear," Ghazal answers.

As the clattering in the kitchen progresses on, Ghazal takes a moment to regain her composure as she walks around the living room and looks at the various framed photos around. Pictures of Qudsia and her husband from their wedding as well as a montage reel of their daughter's different birthday pictures adorn the showcase in the corner which brings a smile to Ghazal's face. And another picture, older and different, that Ghazal can't help but pick up. Of Qudsia in her teens no doubt as she received a distinction award in her school. Ghazal looks at it intently till the clattering in the kitchen begins to die down. Resetting the picture back in its place, Ghazal returns to her sofa as Qudsia returns with a small plate.

"Cookies, fresh out of the oven!"

"Oh dear, you really are spoiling me."

And as both of them indulge in the delightful sugary treats, a tranquil silence takes over. Both of them look at the remaining cookies in their hand, waiting for the other to say something.

"So, uh..." both say at the same time, trying to end the silence, till Ghazal relents.

"It's not a big deal. My husband and I tried, but there were complications and it left me unable to bear any more children. He was alright with it, and just dived himself into his business interests. And me, well I decided to turn my attention to children in general. That's how I got into taking care of other children and well, I never looked back."

"And you've never felt that, I mean, you've never felt the emptiness."

"Emptiness?"

"I mean, God, I can't imagine what my life would be like without my daughter. I know it sounds silly, but sometimes I get the thoughts of what might happen if she weren't there."

"Oh, what a terrible thing to even think of!" Ghazal now becomes a little parental.

"Yeah, it's just a fear I have," Qudsia takes a deep breath. "Actually, I'm an orphan."

Ghazal's earlier frosty response at Qudsia's statement changes instantly on hearing this new bit of information.

"Oh my dear, I never realized..."

"It's alright," Qudsia looks down. "Of course, how could you know?"

"I can't even begin to imagine what you must have felt like. Sure, I worked closely with organizations that took such children in, but I could never really, truly know what it feels like."

"Yeah, you're right. No one else can. And as far as I can remember, I've been at a home for orphans. They were very kind people and never let me feel the absence of my parents. Not that it mattered since I never knew any of my parents. I guess I was abandoned there as soon as I was born."

"How awful," Ghazal remarks.

"Like I said, it didn't matter. I didn't let it stop me from having a normal life, or as normal as you could have in four walls. We had a structured life, education, etiquette, skills... that's actually where I got an interest in baking."

"Oh?"

"Yeah, I guess it was meant to be," Qudsia smiles again. "Everyone had their talents, sewing, gardening, painting; and

I guess this was mine. We had so many events and I used to help out in bake sales to help fund the children's home. We did well for ourselves and didn't want much. Except for maybe every now and then a *home* of our own."

Ghazal can't help but look down as her finger holds on to a half-bitten cookie she can no longer bring herself to finish.

"Some of us would leave, you know," Qudsia continues. "Some would run away but they'd come back eventually. Whether it was finding life outside harsh or just not being able to let go of the home, I don't know. And some would be adopted and we'd never hear from them again. I guess they're happy in their world, but we were happy with ours by the blessings of Allah."

"Indeed."

"And I guess if my life hadn't been this way, I wouldn't have met my future husband. He was an intern with an international aid organization and we were around the same age. We worked together and looked after the new intake of kids, took part in various social events, till eventually he got into a steady job and proposed to me. I guess you could say this was my fairytale come true."

"That does sound magical."

"It does. And yet sometimes I wonder if it would have been perfect if my *actual* parents were there to give me away. If I was able to cry on the shoulders of my real father or if my actual mother had blessed me instead of my family at the home."

"Well, given what you've told me, you didn't need a biological relation to have a family of your own. And in a way, they were more of a family to you than your real parents would ever have been."

"Yeah, you're right. I mean, you know exactly what you're talking about. Because obviously, why would *you* bother to be there..."

Qudsia now looks up at Ghazal, who seems to be taken aback slightly.

"... *mother?*"

On hearing the word, Ghazal's face turns ashen white, her eyes stare wide and her mouth agape. Realizing her face has lost its luster, she tries to bring back the color in her cheeks and hesitates while speaking.

"I... I... I'm sorry. What are you trying to say?"

"You can deny it all you like; it doesn't make a difference to the truth. I mean, I've known it was you all along, all these years since you started visiting the home. I didn't realize it at first in the beginning, when you took a particular interest in me. You'd be nice to me at first, and then for some reason you'd start finding faults in the things I did. Even scolded me in front of everyone and made it a point to praise everyone except me. It was odd, and yeah it hurt. But I just shrugged it away because you weren't there all the time."

"Listen," Ghazal tries to steer this conversation away, "this is all very fanciful, but..."

"But like you said, I do like to do my due diligence. And with technology, I could look up people and find out what they did. Took a while with the slow internet at the home, but I found out about you and the work you did."

"Look child, I honestly don't understand what you're getting at. Sure I may have been around your home at some time, but really I used to do that for so many in the country. And it's pretty likely we may have crossed paths, but there were so many children I met. I can't remember every one of them."

"Yeah, but I have a feeling you did your best to remember me."

"I see," Ghazal scoffs. "And what other things do you know about me?"

"You're a messy eater," Qudsia replies bluntly.

"Excuse me?" Ghazal can't help but chuckle at this out-of-the-blue statement.

"You were at another bake sale recently. We didn't meet but I saw you, doing your best to encourage the other kids, enjoying yourself along with your friends. But you did leave a lot of leftover cakes there, with plenty of your DNA."

"Okay, that's enough!" Ghazal begins to sound agitated while Qudsia sounds completely calm.

"It was more than enough for a maternity test. Enough for me to find out what I needed to know. To *confirm* what I suspected."

"I think we're done here!" Ghazal says brusquely as she gets up and heads for the door. But halfway through, her steps slow down till she reaches a halt. Then she turns around, her head hanging off her shoulders and her eyes looking down at the floor till finally returning to the sofa.

With a deep breath, deeper than she could muster, Ghazal looks back up at Qudsia.

"When did you find out?" Ghazal asks, resigned to her fate.

"Like I said, I only guessed. But in my defense, you were stalking me a lot. So I decided to stalk you back, find out more about you. You obviously never noticed me when I grew up, and I got to hear from different sources about you and your history. I found out how your first pregnancy had complications and that you've never been able to conceive ever since. But it wasn't your *first* pregnancy, was it?"

"No. No it certainly wasn't."

"That's all I know," Qudsia says as she leans back on the sofa, now awaiting a response from Ghazal, who is contemplating just how to start.

"Your father and I, that is, before I got married, we had a fling. We were madly infatuated with each other, so much so I never saw clearly what was happening. Till eventually when his true colors emerged and he abandoned me, leaving me with you growing in me. My parents hushed it all up, but I didn't want to abandon you. I had hoped once you were born, maybe he would come back."

"Right, so that's what I was," Qudsia smirks harshly. "A mistake."

Ghazal's silence is deafening as she is at a loss for words.

"I should go and get the tea,"

Qudsia heads back to the kitchen to pour the tea in the cups and bring it to the table, as if the past few minutes hadn't even happened. Setting the tray on the table, she takes her cup in a saucer and returns to her sofa, leaning back again. Meanwhile, Ghazal stays unmoved.

"After you were born," Ghazal continues, "I didn't know what it was till I later found out about postpartum depression. I was unhappy, but more to the point, my family was unhappy. I had no choice but to think of what was best for me. And in a way, what was best for you too."

"No choice, that's original."

"Think about it. There was no way my family would support my decision. They had a suitor waiting for me, but they wouldn't accept you. No one in their right mind would accept a child born out of wedlock no matter how noble they might appear to be. And really, you had no future with me."

"That's a good one too. Must have been comforting enough to get a good night's sleep."

"Don't judge me!" Ghazal retorts with hurt pride.

"I'll do what I want!" Qudsia replies calmly while sipping her tea. "It's not like you're my mother or anything."

Ghazal's eyes turn red trying to hold back the tears as Qudsia hurls daggers at her.

"So you thought you would come to me and what? That I would let you be a part of my life? That you could be a part of my *daughter's* life."

"She's my granddaughter. I deserve to be part of her life."

"Do you? Just because we share the same blood, doesn't entitle you to walk out of and walk back into my life whenever you like. And it certainly doesn't entitle you to decide that you want to be there for my daughter now because..."

"I know what I did to you was wrong," Ghazal begins to plead. "It was unforgivable. But I tried to make amends. I suffered for what I did to you, how I could never have children again. And after the pregnancy failed, I would have done anything to get you back."

"Yeah, except actually *take* me with you."

"I told you, it wouldn't have worked. My husband..."

"So you decided to be my shadow. Be around every time you were hit with pangs of guilt. You probably said to yourself *'God I wish I had kids, oh I know! Let's go to that home where my actual flesh and blood daughter is and be part of her life for ninety seconds.'*"

The silence is only stifled by the sounds of Qudsia sipping her tea and the cup clinking with the saucer but nevertheless, Ghazal had no answer.

"I just," Ghazal tries to reason with Qudsia, "I just want to be part of your lives. To know you, to make up for all the hurt I've caused. I just need to be there for you and her because it's something that must be done. Because I couldn't stand not being a part of your lives. I just want us to be a real family."

"Oh you don't have to worry about us," Qudsia sets her cup on the table and sounds assertive. "We are a real family. More than you ever were to me, and much more than you could ever hope to be. I hope you enjoyed the cookies and samosas. Do tell your friends."

Dejected, Ghazal gets up from the sofa and walks slowly towards the door. And once again, she stops halfway, only turning her neck towards her daughter.

"'Qudsia.' That is a beautiful name." Ghazal says, her voice breaking under the pressure of her tears. "I wonder who chose it for you."

And with that, Ghazal walks past the front door and closes it behind her as Qudsia watches her mother walk out of her life for the first and no doubt the last time. Once the door is shut, Qudsia holds her face in her palms as she can no longer hold back her tears.

<u>06</u>

BALANCE

The door knob turns and Nada enters her bedroom all exhausted, if the casual way she dumps her handbag on the nearby swivel chair is anything to go by. Removing her earbuds and putting her phone on the charger, she takes off her office coat and work ID card, dumping them unceremoniously over the handbag.

She looks at her tired face in the mirror and the disheveled shirt after a long hard day at work, and simply hangs her head backwards. Walking around aimlessly in the room, she stares first at the ceiling and then at the A/C, which she promptly turns on upon noticing its upturned vents. Once the A/C begins blowing out the chilling Freon-produced air, Nada gazes at the pile she's created on her swivel chair till the laptop on her desk catches her eye.

"Oh, shit!"

Quickly lifting the lid up, she checks that the machine is fully charged and actually on standby. Once she gets the screen up, she notices the two missed video calls on her screen from ten minutes ago.

"Shit, shit, *shit!*"

While she attempts to make the video call, Nada heads back to the mirror to make sure she looks a bit more presentable by running a hairbrush through her straight but dyed brown hair, freshening up a bit of her make-up, and of course, leaving the top button of her shirt open for a bit of cleavage. Just the way *he* likes it.

Nada returns to the laptop screen beaming with a big hundred watt smile, but so far has not received any response at the other end. Thinking that disconnecting and trying again would somehow miraculously get her connected to her fiancé at the other end, she tries again while the rictus smile remains etched on her face. Another minute later, and the smile finally turns upside down to form a frown.

Dejected, Nada closes the laptop lid and heads for the shower. Over the past year they've been engaged, she's noticed her fiancé Sameer has been a lot more possessive and domineering at times, especially when it comes to her. The fact that he's been away for a month to oversee the launching of his company's new business interests seems to have intensified his overprotectiveness of Nada, particularly as her own work commitments have a tendency of keeping her in the office overnight if required. Even letting her work is a lot for Sameer to digest, considering he's always tried to constrict her ambitions in the workplace. Nevertheless, Nada continued to push on and managed to keep his restraint at bay vis-à-vis her career, as she sees a bit of his jealous side every now and then.

Looking at the time of nine-thirty on her charging phone, she realizes it would be half past five in the UK, which means Sameer would be free as a bird to talk to her at the moment. Working it out in her head while she prepares to enter the running shower, Nada realizes he must have called her first thing after he got off from work; not realizing the traffic in Karachi could be rather unforgiving. It was also one of his rules, Nada recalled, that she always answer the video call on her laptop at home so he could get her at a wider angle, and not with the jittery portrait mode of her smartphone while she's out of the house. Just one of the many ways that would – on careful inspection – appear to be a bit more dictatorial; but not to Nada. To her, Sameer's possessiveness and overprotectiveness is only out of love for her and her well-being.

With the moderately cool water washing her tiredness away, she thinks back to when they were first introduced by a mutual friend. Back then, she had just started her job at her present employer after a depressing breakup with a previous boyfriend. Considering how her aim was to have the finer things in life, having a partner who was struggling to make ends meet for his own family seemed to hold no future for her own self. That all changed when she was introduced to Sameer and – much like her start at the new company – the new relationship held a lot of promise as she could now indulge herself in a proper social life without having to worry about who would pick up the check at the restaurant. Not that she couldn't afford it with her new job; it's just that Sameer had far more pride to let his belle pay for him.

Drying herself out of the shower and getting into her night clothes, Nada checks the laptop once again for any more missed video calls, despite being certain she didn't hear any while in the shower. She also checks her phone to see she has no other alerts apart from the receipt for the cab she took home today.

"Tsk, *yaar* you can be such a baby sometimes!"

Nada sends another video call request to Sameer, shaking her head in amazement. It does happen sometimes that he tends to take things personally and is no doubt ignoring her calls out of some misplaced notion that he's punishing her. Nada knows this, and all it takes is a little bit of pandering and pampering to get him back on track, but for now she's going to have to deal with him ignoring her for a few minutes. That is, till the laptop finally beeps as it reaches Sameer's machine at the other end, jerking Nada out of her reverie.

"Finally! Where have you been?"

There's no answer from the other end as the screen appears black, obviously the video feature has been disabled. But Nada knows he's there, since she can hear some noise in the background. This is the first time he's disabled his video, and she thinks he's in one of his *moods*.

"Oh come on, yaar! Don't give me the silent treatment. You know how traffic is in Karachi. It's not like I can just zip around like you can in London. Over here, every hour is rush hour."

Still no answer and the screen stays black. At least she's content he can see her, with her pink powdered cheeks and dimples courtesy of the hundred watt smile she's radiating.

"So have you had dinner? Oh wait, still not dinner time where you're at. Hi-tea then? I don't know about you, but I could murder a pizza right now. All I had for tea was a samosa or two and now I'm just dying to eat something. Since mom went to Islamabad for the conference, I'm usually at home alone till dad gets back from work. Sometimes I just see him for breakfast. The cook has probably made some daal chaawal but I'm going to have that and the pizza. Creamy tikka, your favorite flavor. Wouldn't you like some?"

At this point, Nada may as well be offering a slice to her laptop if it could eat anything, since Sameer has been inconspicuously quiet. With nothing flickering on the screen or the speakers save for the background noise, Nada's cheeks begin to hurt from the smile as it begins to recede back.

"You do know that long distance calls aren't like they used to be, right? Mom keeps telling me in her whole grandma voice about how they had to use hundred-rupee calling cards to make international calls. That sounds so depressing, and I guess they would value the little bit of time those calling cards could get you by talking about everything on their minds. Meanwhile, here you are with such technology at your fingertips, and you're just being... come *on*! What do you want me to say? You think I was ignoring you? I've got the cab receipt with the time it dropped me off if you don't believe me."

Just then, the screen comes to life with the familiar background of Sameer's hotel room. But Nada is taken aback at the face that is *not* of her fiancé. Staring back at her is another man with long hair till his earlobes, a neatly trimmed beard and dark brown eyes. While she is shocked to see an absolute stranger sitting where his fiancé should be, she doesn't feel threatened considering his face is rather gentle and kind, if a little weary and hardened.

"I'm sorry," the stranger answers back, "I didn't realize I had accepted the call by mistake. I was just trying to turn the laptop off but then you just went on. The video over here was already disabled, apparently."

"No it's..."

Nada tries to regain her bearings as she ties her flowing hair with a clip and straightens her shirt, taking care to close the upper button for modesty's sake.

"I'm sorry, but who are you? And why are you answering my fiancé's laptop?"

"Oh, you're Sameer's *fiancé*? I had no idea he was engaged. He neglected to mention that to me while we were talking."

"Right, and again, you are?"

"Sorry, where are my manners? I'm Javed. Sameer and I, uh, we know each other from college."

"Oh, really?" Nada seems a bit more relaxed now. "You're friends?"

"Uh, not really," Javed replies, his expression more pleasant. "Well, not for a while considering he never kept in touch, never mind letting me know he got engaged."

"That's weird. It was a pretty big engagement party right here in Karachi last year. I'm surprised he didn't invite you considering he had a lot of friends over."

"Yeah, but then again I do travel a lot for my work. And I haven't been in Karachi quite some time. Besides which, like I said, we haven't been in touch since college."

"Right, well it's nice to meet you, Javed. My name is Nada."

"I know."

"You do?" Nada is a little alarmed. "How? You said he never told you about me."

"It's written right here on the screen."

"Oh, right!" Nada hits her forehead with her palm at the faux pas. "That, was dumb."

"There's a little blue heart next to it, too."

"It's blue topaz, actually. My birthstone color. I set up the contact on his laptop myself. I'm so glad he hasn't changed it."

"What does that even mean, by the way? Your name?"

"Generous."

"Nice. I guess Sameer's quite lucky to have found you."

"Let's just say the feeling is mutual. We were both meant to be, and we have a great connection together."

"Really? Because it didn't sound like that earlier."

"Huh?" Nada looks a bit caught off-guard.

"Well, what you were saying before I activated the camera here, you sounded as if he would be angry at you for being late with your call, at least that's what I gathered. And it also seemed like he's been like this before, wanting to be pampered into forgiving you."

"Excuse me?" Nada sounds a bit irritated.

"Right, my bad. I think I'm overreaching myself a bit, since it's none of my business commenting on your personal life."

"You're right," Nada sounds stern with her arms folded, "it isn't. Besides, what are you even doing over there with his laptop? Isn't he at home?"

"Oh he uh, he just had to go out. I was making myself at home when you called and I'm rather clumsy with technology for my sins, so before you knew it, here we are."

"Right."

Nada takes a deep breath, still not exactly sure of Javed aside from the fact that he doesn't seem to be all that bad. Or as bad as any of Sameer's friends she knew. Which leads her to wonder.

"You know, you don't seem like one of his friends. I mean, I've met most of his friends and you're not like them. You're more, uh..."

"Middle-class?" Javed retorts casually.

"No!" Nada smirks a little out of embarrassment, "I meant nice. Or humble. Both, actually. You're not as full of yourself as him. *Them!* I meant them."

"Well, guess that hasn't changed. You're right, though. I guess it's why we didn't stay in touch all this time. He could be a bit of an influencer."

For the first time, Nada seems to have an expression of understanding on her face, almost as if she could relate to everything said by this man she has never met before. Not only that, she is beginning to find the kind of insights into his fiancé she has casually been keeping buried down with her feelings of love for him.

"You know, when you said that stuff before, about him wanting me to apologize..."

"Yeah, I guess that was out of line. I'm so sorry for having said that."

"No, it's uh, it's okay. You weren't actually so far off."

"Oh?"

"Yeah, I've found he could be a little, you know, *possessive*."

"Oh, right. Yeah."

"Oh hang on," Nada just realizes, "since you were with him in college, you must know about, well, you know, *other* girlfriends of his, right?"

"Ah, yeah, um, I don't think I should be..."

"Oh come on!" Nada sounds positively reassuring, if a bit inquisitive. "You don't have to worry about embarrassing him."

"Well, I'm not concerned about that. I just didn't want *you* to feel embarrassed."

"Seriously, it's the twenty-first century. I'm sure an outgoing guy like him must have had his fair share of girlfriends."

"And that doesn't bother you?"

"Why should it? I mean, before I met Sameer, I ended a relationship with another guy, so there. And anyways, he's never made any bones about it. You know, *'there's just too many to remember all the names right now...'* yadda yadda!"

"Well, I wouldn't know about an exact number, but yeah, they varied. There was this one he was really into. And I mean *really* into. So much so that any other guy caught talking to her would get beat up."

"No way!"

"I remember this one guy who got caught, and Sameer and his *gang* beat him up. No one helped the poor guy."

"Is that true?" Nada sounds a bit apprehensive.

"I was there. I saw it all happen. That's not even the half of it. After kicking him around a bit, they put him inside some cage that was supposed to be there for a water motor. The motor was out for repairs or something. Anyways, once they caged him in, Sameer decided it would be fun to shock him with a taser."

"What? No, that can't be true."

"Sorry. I shouldn't have said anything..."

"No it's just... wait..."

And then it hits her.

"You said you were there. Did you..."

"Oh no," Javed shrugs, "I wasn't in his gang. Merely a witness. And a *victim*."

"What?"

"We weren't *exactly* friends, if I'm being honest. And Sameer wasn't exactly a saint. In fact, he got a kick out of bullying people. The only reason he never got expelled was because his father was some big-shot. Anyways, once his fury was satiated with tasing that other guy, his gang decided it would be fun to torture me because I was a bit overweight at the time. I was able to break the taser apart before they could use it on me, but that just made things worse."

"That's... you're making this up!"

"It wasn't the first time. It wouldn't be the last. I mean sure, if it were just me and him, we'd probably beat the shit out of each other in a fair fight. But he didn't believe in fairness, and he certainly relied a lot on his friends to hold his victims down while he beat them up and then urinated on."

Nada's face instantly recoils at this new bit of information.

"You're lying. He's not like that at all."

Javed takes a deep breath and looks back at the screen sympathetically.

"Look, you seem like a decent enough person, so I'm sorry if what I said makes you uncomfortable. And maybe he might have changed too. But the person I knew was an abusive bully and sadist who relished in tormenting and humiliating anyone and everyone he disliked. And it wasn't just physical degradation, but also mental. The poor guy who got tasered ended up vanishing away from society and living in seclusion. Everyone else had to get therapy. And I don't even want to comment on the girls he slept around with in his one night stands."

"Stop, please!"

Nada massages her temples and gets up from the chair. Looking at herself in the mirror again, she appears as if she's been running a marathon for over an hour in just a few minutes it took for Javed to make all these revelations.

Returning to her chair, she sees that Javed looks a bit perturbed as well. At first, she assumed it was because of regret for making her feel terrible by telling her all of

Sameer's previous indiscretions. But soon enough, she began to empathize as she realized Javed must have had a hard time reliving all those moments and incidents of violence at Sameer's hands.

If it were all *true*, that is.

"Look, it's getting late and I have to go to work in the morning. Just tell Sameer I called him once he gets back. I'm sure we'll have a lot to talk about."

"Oh, that's not possible. I'll be leaving in a little bit actually and lock the door on the way out."

"That's okay, you can just leave a note on the laptop and mention it. He'll read it once he gets back."

"No, you misunderstand," Javed's voice sounds a lot more sincere than ever before. "Sameer's not coming back here. He's never coming back."

"What?" Nada looks perplexed. "Why not?"

"Because I *killed* him while you were calling him before."

Nada's face stood frozen, but her eyes widen in horror at what Javed just said. Her mouth moves as if to say *'what?'* but there is no voice due to the shock.

"Well, actually, I beat him to death."

"N-n-n-no, that, that's not..." Nada is just stuttering now. "You're lying."

"You know how I mentioned all those people he victimized. How they all entered therapy or cut themselves out of society or had to spend the rest of their lives looking over their shoulders? You know what else they had in common? They moved on with their lives. A little broken and messed up, sure. But alive, which is more than I can say for one or two of the girls who ended up running away from home or overdosing themselves on drugs, or worse. And then there was *me*."

Nada's silence doesn't mean much to Javed anymore, who just continues to unburden himself.

"See, I made a mistake. I wasn't a violent person, but my hatred continued to fester over getting even with him even after every beating and every humiliation I endured. But no matter what I tried, I couldn't win. That just made the abuse worse every time. There was no balance in our encounters. It was just him getting the better of me and treating me like dog shit. Till eventually my grades slipped and I had to run away. I had no more prospects left till I ended up doing questionable things. You know, petty thievery, extortion, beating people up for a living. One thing led to another and before you knew it, I ended up joining an international gang of criminals. I wasn't in the upper levels, but my job was just committing violence against my targets. Eventually, I graduated to killing for hire. Amazing how life can mess you up. I actually wanted to be an artist."

Javed looks away a little as he spots the glistening tears gathering in Nada's eyes.

"Please, stop!" Nada pleads.

"Okay, I understand. It was nice talking to you."

"No, please. Just stop lying. You didn't kill him. Why, why would you kill him?"

Javed closes his eyes and opens them up again, this time appearing serious.

"Purely business. I was tasked to kill him because of his dealings with my clients. Or rather, his *losing* my clients' money. See, he was dealing with some of the criminal elements in his finances, and he was using the money to fund his own lavish lifestyle. He thought he had gotten away, but my organization has eyes everywhere. It just so happened that I got word for killing him. Now you might think we get encrypted pictures of our targets, but usually the easiest way is to have them pointed out. And the moment I saw him coming out of his hotel, the moment my partner pointed him out, I was just speechless. There he was, bright as day! His acne had gone and he looked a bit more well-groomed, but there was no mistaking him with all his self-assuredness and swagger. Finally, after all these years. Finally, I could have balance."

"It... it..." Nada manages to wipe away her tears, "it was all years ago. Surely you couldn't have been holding a grudge that long."

"Oh but it's *exactly* what I had been doing. Besides which, I was hired to do a job. It just became a lot more fun. If I'm honest, I just didn't know what the icing on the cake was. The fact that I would finally have him right where I wanted him, or the fact that I was getting paid a good deal of money for it."

"I don't believe you."

"Why ever not?"

"Because you're not a horrible person. You're not a criminal. You don't sound like one, and you and Sameer could just be playing some sick joke on me."

Nada sounded so sure of herself that Javed looks down and shakes his head.

"Well yeah, I mean I am pretty soft-spoken for a hired thug and killer. But see, that doesn't change the facts."

Nada is then horrified at what she sees next, as Javed raises his fists up to his face. Both his hands are taped in white, covered in the crimson of blood.

"And the facts are simple: I hurt people. I kill people. Occasionally I hurt the people I kill, and kill the people I hurt. And if it hasn't become any clear to you, I *really* enjoy doing it. So believe me when I tell you that as I pummeled the life out of your fiancé, as I beat his face black and blue till eventually there was nothing left of it that would mistake it for a human being, I thoroughly enjoyed it. With every punch, with every blow, I evened out every single thing he had put me through. Every humiliation, every single instance of persecution, every vile bit of excrement he had subjected me to."

Javed's cold, calm demeanor continues to terrify Nada, as she covers her open mouth with her hand in shock.

"And if that weren't enough," he continues "I balanced out what he did to all the others: the misguided fools who thought they could get a phone number out of one of his squeezes, the hapless idiots who did nothing more than to park on his spot or refused to let him cheat off of their exams, and all the stupid bitches who thought he loved them all enough to give up their virginities. That's all there is to it."

It's difficult for Javed to read Nada's face at the moment. He could pick out the rage and hatred sure enough, but there were other things he's beginning to piece together. Other emotions Nada is trying her best to hide behind the anger. Nevertheless, Nada took a while to register them all. Sadness, pain, loss... and one more that surprised even her.

Relief.

"So," Nada manages to speak, her teeth now gritting, "what now?"

"Nothing. It's done. While you and I were talking, my partner was removing his body and meticulously scrubbing the crime scene from any evidence of murder, DNA, foul play and what have you. It'll be like we weren't even here. The police will find his body soon enough. The rest is up to you."

"What do you mean?"

"There's a button on your keyboard that'll let you capture an image of me. You could send it to the police, Interpol, whoever. You could tell them you had this conversation, and they'll do some technical forensics to find me. Eventually they'll put me in jail. Been there, done that."

Nada looks down at her keyboard at the Print Screen key, just like he mentioned. She brings her finger over it and looks back at Javed.

"You don't seem afraid. You're not the least bit concerned about what I can do with your picture."

"Why should I? Like I said, it was purely business. And yeah, I got what I wanted after all these years."

"So what's to stop me from notifying the authorities and telling them all about you?"

"You tell me," Javed shrugs.

Nada looks at Javed, at his eyes, at what he believes to be true. She stares at his face, kind, gentle, compassionate, and tries to weigh it all against the feelings she has for Sameer. Or rather had.

"You killed him. You killed the man I... I..."

"Say it."

"The man I ... "

Her volume lowers, but still audible enough to pass through the laptop's microphone."

"... loved."

Even as she says it, she realizes she doesn't believe it. And even Javed can see the truth in her face as he cocks his head.

"So I did. But the question is, *did* you love him though?"

With an uncomfortable silence that seems to last for eternity, Nada's finger continues to hover over the Print Screen button.

"You haven't been lying to me at all," Nada finally asks, "have you?"

"I don't even know you. And besides, I'm a killer. If nothing else, I'm as honest as they come."

With that, Nada moves her finger away from the Print Screen button and towards the track pad. Scrolling the pointer towards the call cancel button, Nada looks intently at Javed again.

"Goodbye."

Javed nods, as Nada finally cuts the call.

Letting out a deep sigh, Nada wipes the tears off of her reddened eyes as she thinks to herself. Then, without a second thought, she makes another video call to Sameer's ID and patiently waits for a response. Her heart beats a bit faster as her smile returns, a bit different and not of her usual brilliance she would make for her fiancé, but one beaming with a genuine bit of optimism and hopefulness. It glows a bit more as the laptop beeps and the screen flickers again.

"Hi!"

STRENGTH

Akram Chaudhary steps back into his office on the twentieth floor, as the sound of the flushing water begins to recede once the door to his personal executive washroom closes behind him. Returning back to his immense mahogany desk while passing by the view of the city skyline from the screen windows, he squirts out some hand sanitizer and rubs vigorously till the sound of the intercom begins to buzz.

"Yes, what is it?" He inquires after picking up the receiver.

The voice on the other crackles faintly and his expression changes to a pleasant one.

"Oh right, of course! Send him in, and send in the hi-tea once it is ready."

Dressed in his trousers, shirt and vest, Akram completes his three-piece ensemble by putting on the blue striped suit jacket from the rack. Giving himself a once-over in the full-length mirror, Akram keenly settles his greyish hair and bushy moustache before turning towards the sound of the main door opening.

"Uh, hello. My name is Ehsan Saleem."

"Ehsan, how delighted to finally meet you!" Akram says with a beaming smile and a cheerful demeanor as he walks over to vigorously shake Ehsan's hand.

"Nice to meet you as well, Mr. Chaudhary."

"Akram, please! No need to stand on ceremony here."

Patting Ehsan's shoulder hard enough for the dark grey suit to cry in agony, Akram leads his guest towards the mahogany desk and asks him to take a seat.

"I hope you don't mind if I took the liberty to order some hi-tea. You like tea, don't you?"

"Of course, and it's your company. You do as you like."

"Yes, well it's been quite a journey for me bringing this whole business up. And I suppose it's been quite a journey for you too, getting to where you are today."

"I don't think that's a fair comparison. You're one of the biggest suppliers of construction material and facilitators for building in the entire country. You have government contracts and a presence all through the four provinces, plus a huge share of the international pie. We're just a bit-player in a fiercely competitive market."

"You are way too modest for your own good, you know," Akram smiles. "Sure your company, uhhh..."

"Prometheus Constructions."

"Right, yes; sure you've just been around for a couple of years, but there are major players out there in your fiercely competitive market that would kill for a fraction of the success you've achieved in such a short time."

"Well that's a credit to our founder and CEO. It was his leadership that brought us along this way."

"Yes, but I don't think that's all. A leader is nothing without the team he leads, and I can't imagine Prometheus could have gotten anywhere without the role you played as the head of business development."

"Just following the course of our leadership," Ehsan smirks. "We have a high-quality product and are dedicated to going the extra mile in our range of services. I just advertise what we have to offer."

"Oh I don't doubt you have something great to sell. Surely all of them out there sell the very best to their clients, as do we. But you? You have the magic tongue that casts a spell over your clients, and a sharp intellect that knows where to strike to achieve your goals. In the past two years, you've come up and managed to snare some of our blue-chip clients. Not the bigger ones, obviously, but your strategy is marvelous."

"How so?" Ehsan cocks his head.

"Do you like roti?" Akram casually asks, making Ehsan squint his eyes in curiosity.

"Uh, of course, everyone does."

"I love bread. It's the thing that breeds life in me. Curiously enough, I tend to eat up the outer ring first, no matter what kind I eat. Chapatis, naans, even sliced bread. It's always the outer rim first before the big centerpiece. Take out the rough edges first and then get to the soft but larger piece."

"I'm sure a lot of people eat it like that," Ehsan smirks again, "myself included. It's neater this way, I guess."

"Exactly!" Akram taps his desk. "It's neater. Just like the strategy you adopted to rope in our clients. You decided to take out the most exposed ones, the ones we don't hold too close to our chests because they're just there to make up numbers. The little ones who swarm around us because of the real money-making clients we have at our core. The government, the public services, the major corporations both domestic and foreign. Those are the ones we really protect, and everyone else beyond that is just there to form the edges.

"Well when you put it like that, I guess it wasn't too hard for us to bring them over to us. They were getting rather tired with your shifting tariffs and delays in delivery. No doubt we couldn't compete with you in terms of price, but we could assure faster delivery and completion time."

"Oh yes, they would like that, wouldn't they? Faster delivery, faster everything. You have to realize in a company our size, things take time and our more lucrative contracts take precedence. We have to make sure *they* continue to stay with us, and therefore ensure all our resources are geared towards them. So naturally, the smaller clients will have to wait a certain time to get what they pay for."

"Right, well I guess it was really your operating procedure that gave us the opportunity to convince them to come with us. So it really was a shortcoming your company could have easily avoided. No offense."

"None taken." Akram motions his hands to express his affability over the whole matter. "It was down to us and we accept we left that window of a golden chance for you to pounce on. But you did something far more unthinkable. You actually convinced them to let go of a market leader and join an unknown and new enterprise. And you cleverly contacted them all with the full knowledge they could easily get out of their contracts with us after paying off a cancellation fee. You actually convinced them so well they'd be better off without us that you actually made them do anything possible to sever ties with us. How on earth did you manage it?"

"Well," Ehsan responds while clearing his throat, "this is where I'll have to act on my obligation to Prometheus and respectfully decline to comment on any ongoing business strategy. It would be a conflict of interest."

"Hehehehe..." Akram chuckles, "sharp as a tack."

Just then, the knock at the door manages to divert the attention of both men.

"Excellent, come!" Akram calls at the door before looking back at Ehsan. "Hope you like the spread. The samosas are to die for."

The tea trolley enters and the valet is about to serve when Ehsan abruptly gets up from his seat and pours a cup of tea for himself from the pot. Akram and the valet can only watch in a bit of amusement as Ehsan stirs the tea and puts a few snacks on a plate. The valet leaves after serving Akram, who watches Ehsan return to his seat with his tea and snacks. No one speaks of what just took place as they sip the tea.

"Prometheus!" Akram exclaims, much to break the silence. "Like the one from Greek myth where he steals fire from the gods for mankind. Very apt of you to choose it."

"Wasn't exactly our first choice when we were founding the company."

"Oh right, yes. You've been there from the very beginning, haven't you?"

"Started off as a junior sales manager, worked my way to the upper levels of the hierarchy. Back then, we all knew what we were doing without an actual organization chart. A year later and well, I'm sure you already did your due diligence on how we rose up."

"Yes, and it is a remarkable feat, mostly because of how you conducted business. But let's face it, you didn't just do it for bringing the company to the forefront. You just wanted to shine a spotlight in the sky for someone to notice your talents and business acumen. Someone high enough to pick you up from the ground and put you up on a higher plane. Well, isn't it?"

"Um, I think you've lost me there."

"Alright, I'll come right out with it then. This whole meeting wasn't just to compliment you on your masterful tactics at taking away my business. This was an interview."

"Excuse me?"

"You really think I don't see through what you've done? All this effort and energy, all this skillfulness at getting clients away solely from my company. What do you think it means?"

"Sound business strategy?" Ehsan remarks. "Hitting the goliath of the industry and taking its clients would make us a force to be reckoned with."

"On the outside, yes. But I know what you want. And I do mean *you*, specifically. This was all just a demonstration, a *résumé* if you will to flaunt in the face of the goliath."

Ehsan doesn't reply as his face appears to be clueless, much to Akram's amusement.

"Yes," Akram smiles wide, "I'd like you, Ehsan Saleem, to come work for me."

"Ah," Ehsan's mouth is wide open as Akram chuckles.

"Now before you say anything, hear me out. I don't know exactly what Prometheus is paying you, not for lack of trying mind you, but I'm certain I can offer you a far more lucrative opportunity. Double the salary you're taking there for a start, along with far more profitable stock options, benefits, bonuses, your own personal house bought and built by us. And the biggest opportunity of all: a chance to rub shoulders with the real power brokers of the industry.

Meeting with some of our worthwhile clients, a foot in the door of all our government, corporate and international contracts. You'd have a field day with them, I'm sure, and would have a chance to bring in newer projects."

"That..." Ehsan ponders, "... is indeed something worth thinking about. But I'm sure your offer works both ways."

"True. You'd have to bring back all the business you took from me for a start. Not to mention all that Prometheus has managed to build. I could just offer to buy the company out, a hostile takeover if you will, but with you I don't need to go into all that until much later. You know the ins and outs of how they operate, so you'd be in a prime position to scuttle them."

"Very shrewd."

"Oh I'm just getting started," Akram continues to smile while sipping his tea. "Once we're done with Prometheus, we will continue to expand aggressively: take over the other up and coming smaller rivals and then begin to consolidate. Make inroads into the other major companies and begin expanding our client base. Mark my words; in the next five years, we'll be the only company that'll be applying for tenders. No one else would even dare."

"Sounds rather monopolistic," Ehsan can't help but comment. "Not to mention a bit vindictive."

"It's business," Akram replies coldly. "Tough steps need to be taken if we're to grow. And believe me, you'd want to be on the winning side."

Akram watches Ehsan take a few calculated sips of tea, obviously indicating he doesn't wish to comment any further.

"Look," Akram leans forward, "don't tell me right now. Sleep on it, talk it over with the family and let me know in a couple of days."

"Actually, I'd rather just tell you right now." Ehsan sets his cup on the coaster. "My answer is no."

"Don't be so rash, Ehsan!" Akram chides.

"No, actually, I *did* have an inkling of why you really wanted to meet me. I'm not exactly an idiot."

"I wouldn't even dream of it."

"I will tell you why I'm saying no," Ehsan continues. "First of all, I don't think you or your company are the right fit for me. You're like a star at the end of its ten-billion year life. Towards the end, it grows and bloats into a red giant with virtually no energy, till at last it ends and turns into a little dwarf. That's just how your company is right now."

"Hmmm," Akram scratches his head. "I've never heard it put like that before."

"Secondly, I'm not a huge fan of your business practices. There were several scandals of abuses in your factories and brick kilns, human rights abuses."

"Well now, that is just tabloid propaganda." Akram leans back. "I'm surprised you've fallen for that. You know how it is: investigative journalists who have nothing better to report resort to slander of all kinds."

"I'm sure they do, but I've actually come across such stories for a fact. And I've looked into *your* background as well."

"Pardon?" Akram raises an eyebrow.

"I'm sure the suit and western grooming is all well and good, but back then in your formative years, you were just a run-of-the-mill feudal landowner whose father had decided to get into brick kilns as the next big thing. And much like your father and his dealings in agriculture, you didn't fall far from the tree with your ruthlessness and iron-fisted tactics against your workers. Meager pays, inhumane living conditions, and even subjecting children to laboring as slaves. You even had them all kept in dungeons and set dogs on them if they didn't comply or tried to escape. Not that any of them could, what with all the high fences and barbed wire surrounding your compound."

"That's very imaginative."

"I thought so too, but reality often can be quite cruel. I've heard it all, you know, from the ones who were lucky enough to escape. Those who could no longer endure being at your boot heel. How those who tried to escape would be caught and then whipped brutally by not just the foremen, but by you personally. And you started doing so even before you reached your teens. Men, women, children, horses... apparently you had a penchant for whipping everything like they were mules."

On hearing all this, Akram just shakes his head and claps a little in amusement.

"Well, what can I say?"

"You don't deny it?" Ehsan asks.

"What would be the point? True or not, you've already made up your mind about me. Whoever spoke to you and told you that entire sob-story, whatever brainwashing they've done, well they've succeeded. Funny because I thought you were the convincing genius. Looks like even you can be swayed. But then, it just occurs to me why you even bothered coming here. If you had an idea of why I'd called you, you could have found an excuse to meeting a, hehe..."

Akram raises his hands in the air and motions inverted quotations with his fingers.

"A *horrible person* like me. A slave master, if you will."

"Well, that was the idea all along of course. I had to come here to meet you, to have this meeting."

"Right, you didn't want to insult me over the phone and instead decided to do it in person. Now who's being ruthless and vindictive?"

"No, I'm sorry, I wasn't clear. I actually wanted to meet you personally, to show you who I was, what I had become. To meet with you on equal terms, or at least as equal as I could get to be in your presence. But I got something better. Because I wasn't the one who initiated this meeting. You did. You called me here. You were *forced* to meet me."

At this, it's Akram's turn now to appear a little clueless.

"I don't understand. Why did you want to meet me?"

"Because all that I told you, all that had happened in the past, all the things you've done are as true as you and I. They're certainly not something I needed to be brainwashed about."

"Well, I thought you had already made your mind up about it."

"True," Ehsan lets out a deep breath and pulls up the left sleeve of his jacket and opens the cuff button on his shirt, "but I do have my reasons."

Curious about Ehsan's latest act, Akram looks towards the unbuttoned cuff, but Ehsan makes it easier for him to look. Akram's rises up from his seat a bit to peer over, but his eyes open wide in horror at the sight of the number "61" branded right into the skin of Ehsan's forearm.

"Dear God!" Akram's mouth is open as he drops into his seat and holds onto the arms of the chair. "You can't, you can't be..."

"My name is Ehsan Saleem. I was born in your ancestral village. More to the point, I was born in the very same dungeon you kept my mother, father, and three older sisters. I received this brand on my very first birthday to ensure I would be bound to you. My mother told me I cried for weeks and was lucky to be alive. My parents were too old fashioned to understand any life outside of servitude to you but eventually; as they all saw how brutal you and your clan had become, we made a break for it. My father didn't survive, but the rest of us were lucky. I was only five years old when I saw him die. You were well into your teens when you shot him from a distance in your jeep."

"No, it's not possible!"

"We had help, of course. There are people in this world who work hard to liberate those subjected to cruelties like us. They helped us disappear and make new lives for ourselves. But we would never truly be free of you, not where it really mattered. We would still be your slaves in mind if not in body, so we began the process of becoming better. We went to school, learned to read, worked hard, received opportunities that were otherwise unavailable to us. We became who we are today. My eldest sister is a surgeon, the other two are teachers. And me?"

Ehsan finally stands up and leans forward with his hands on the desk, causing Akram to recoil just a bit.

"I made it my life's purpose to be tougher, more capable and more of a force than you could ever be. I wanted to stand in front of you, face you in the eye and have you pander to me, beg me to help you. Beg me: a *lesser* being in your mind, to be your partner. To help you regain your fortunes. I just wanted to prove that you are not a god. You are just like me, flesh and blood. Given the right opportunities, people like me could reach their full potential were it not for vicious and pitiless people like you and your clans-folk."

"So all this," Akram finally speaks, his throat choking a bit with sweat gathering on his forehead, "you and Prometheus, taking our clients, it was all just a slap at my face?"

"You could say that. But above else, it was a declaration. We have laborers certainly, but we provide fairness to them in ways you couldn't even comprehend. We don't terrorize the people who work for us into submission. Their children go to schools, their kin receive the best healthcare we can provide them."

"You really don't think you've won, do you?" Akram finally gets up, appearing a bit more confident. "You think you'll be able to defeat us?"

"I don't need to," Ehsan straightens up and adjusts his jacket. "You're more than capable of running your business into the ground yourself once the harsh conditions of your mega-enterprise become known. It might not be today, or tomorrow, or for years to come. But sooner or later, you'll be the cause of your own destruction.

Akram just smirks as Ehsan smiles back.

"As for me? I just need to be nothing like you."

"When you went to pick up the cup of tea yourself..." Akram registers some realization in his face, "you were *empathizing* with my valet?"

"I'm more than capable of not relying on someone else to do my bidding. I'm stronger this way. Good day, Mr. Chaudhary."

With a confident stride in his step, Ehsan Saleem walks away as Akram Chaudhary looks on in disgust, no longer able to hide the hatred from appearing on his face.

<u>08</u>

SALVATION

"So that's how many cartons of milk again?"

Dr. Faisal walks down the corridor jotting down some notes on his clipboard, while his smartphone is wedged between his left ear and shoulder as he manages to continue the conversation and note down some important items he'll need to pick up on the way home later. Wearing a white lab coat over a light blue kameez and shalwar – the latter having the unmistakable remnants of mud stains – he clicks the pen off and pockets it before adjusting his spectacles around his graying temples.

"I still don't see why you couldn't text me all this, or leave a voice message."

The response at the other end leaves a grimace in his face.

"Of course I don't have you on mute! You're my wife. I couldn't mute you even if I wanted to."

He must have realized even before he said it that he would regret it.

"No, of course that's not what I want. I don't hate your voice. Look, can we discuss this when I get home, okay. I'll be sure to get the stuff."

The audible crackling of the phone does no favors to the Doctor's grimace.

"Of course, I've written it all down. I'm putting it in my pocket as well. Take care."

And with that, he finally cuts the call and places the phone in his side pocket. Even after the call has been disconnected, his head is still a bit tilted towards the left and his shoulder is hunched. Apparently he has made a habit of taking calls like this quite a lot and for far more prolonged periods.

Eventually, he arrives at his destination, a room labeled simply as CONFERENCE. Once he enters and locks the door from the inside, he can't help but notice the dim lights he rectifies soon by switching on the rest from the switchboard.

"Well, hello there," the doctor declares. "And how is our star patient today?"

Dr. Faisal takes a seat in front of the small conference table, across from which sits another man in a straightjacket. The doctor takes in the patient's ragged appearance, his overgrown and unkempt grey hair and beard, his eyes drained and his cheeks drooping from the despair of his incarceration."

"I must say, you've looked better than this. You should be letting us take better care of you. You could do with a quick shave and trim. And what's this I hear about you refusing your meals?"

The doctor clicks his tongue, obviously dismayed at the state of his patient's condition.

"Proper nutrition is vital if you want to stay in shape. If there's a problem with the present meals, we could arrange something different. Whatever makes you feel comfortable."

The patient finally looks up at the doctor, his eyes crying out both with sadness and anger.

"Let me out of here!"

"Now, now," the doctor makes notes in his clipboard, "that is not how we ask for things, remember?"

The patient lowers his eyes and sniffles just a little.

"Let me out of here ... *please.*"

"There, that's better. And *no*, you know full well you can't leave. You're here for a reason, in fact, letting you out would cause far more harm than good to the society."

"I don't mean any harm to society."

"Really?" the Doctor shakes his head and his tone begins to get sterner. "You still refuse to acknowledge what you've done to them? All the suffering and all the pain you've caused to virtually everyone you've touched. Do you want to put them through all that again?"

Hearing the Doctor's elevated voice, the patient begins to retreat back into his cocoon as his head tries to go back inside his body like a turtle in its shell. The doctor, realizing his mistake, changes his tone to a more apologetic one.

"I'm ... I'm sorry. I'm so sorry. I should know better than to be harsh. Water?"

With that, Dr. Faisal pushes forward a sippy cup with a straw sticking out towards the patient, taking care to stay away from around the patient who begins to come out of his shell and sips uncomfortably from the straw.

"Perhaps later we can get you something good to eat. Some fast food, maybe?"

Hearing a more sympathetic tone from the doctor, the patient begins to nod his head.

"Barbecue?"

"Yes, why not?" Dr. Faisal smiles. "What did you have in mind?"

"Behari boti."

"Good choice, now that you mention it. Beef?"

The patient nods.

"Excellent. See? This is brilliant progress."

As the doctor scribbles some more notes, the patient takes a few more sips of water. Even with his head tilted a little to the side, Dr. Faisal notices the desperation and can't help but take a deep breath.

"I had such great admiration for you once," the doctor sighs. "I mean all those pictures and videos of you when you came back to the country with that trophy. It wasn't just that. I mean all the people who cheered with excitement. They were so over the moon when you came back."

The patient looks at the doctor for a few seconds before speaking.

"You must have been very young."

"Oh, yes. I think I heard it on the radio when you won. My father was very elated. I've even heard one of my youngest aunts was so crazy about you that she ran away from home just to find you. We found her soon enough, though."

"That must have been relieving."

"Yes well, like you said, I was young. What did I know?"

The doctor continues scribbling his notes.

"It was even a big deal when you decided to run for government. It was almost fitting, a world champion athlete leading the nation, and your agenda for cleaning up corruption was revolutionary. I voted for you, you know. I had such high hopes."

Dr. Faisal sighs as he adjusts his spectacles.

"Oh well, lamenting over the past doesn't do any good. We must all look to the future, right?"

"Why isn't your head up straight, doctor?" The patient says, noticing the doctor's head.

"Excuse me?" The doctor looks puzzled. In his line of work, it's usually the other person whose head isn't up straight.

"Your head," the patient replies. "It's leaning on the side."

"Oh, right yes. Force of habit, I guess. I travel by bike so I take my calls while riding. I've got to have it between my ear and shoulder if I'm to hold onto the handlebars.

"But... isn't it dangerous? Don't you wear a helmet?"

"In this weather?" The doctor scoffs.

"You're a *doctor*. You should be more careful."

"Well I never needed helmets before. Actually I had a car. Small one, but was pretty useful. Till the prices of fuel kept going up and up, and the banks would keep revising their interest rates. Eventually, I couldn't afford to pay for the lease and they repossessed it. Good thing, I suppose. The cleaner was charging me a fortune!"

Dr. Faisal leans back a little in his chair, glaring at the patient.

"As for helmets, well with all the imports blocked, there aren't any helmets available. All the local helmet manufacturers folded up because they couldn't keep paying taxes, that is if the shortfall in power and gas didn't put them out of business. For that matter, most local businesses began shutting down. None of them even knew what tax meant, and all of a sudden anyone earning a little bit of money owed the government tax."

"All income is subject to tax." The patient tries to answer.

"Tell that to the street vendors who sell burgers or French fries, or the cobbler who sits outside in the heat mending shoes. Or the fruit and vegetable vendors who make just about enough to not have to eat their own merchandise. Do you think they're the kind of people who owe taxes to the government?"

"It's the law. Everyone is subject to it."

"Don't I know it! I swear if this keeps up, the government is going to have more money than what to do with. Say what you will about how clean and non-corrupt this lot is from the previous governments, but all that treasure should be pretty tantalizing to even the most pious of them."

"They have done some good work. Look at how the trash problem is being solved."

"Well, that is quite the debate. I mean, yes this city and other parts of the country could do with the cleanup. But I'll admit I was very skeptical about this plan. I mean, who would have thought it? The government couldn't clamp down on plastic shopping bags, but they then made it obligatory to add holy verses on all sorts of plastic wrappers. No one would ever dare throw them on the street knowing they'd be committing holy desecration. I'd probably call it revolutionary if it weren't just too stupid at face value."

"It worked, didn't it? People stopped throwing shopping bags, wrappers and packets on the streets."

"True, but then there's the problem. What were they going to do with all the wrappers and packaging piling up in their household? Avoiding eternal damnation is one thing, but pretty soon every house was brimming with trash. I had boxes upon boxes sent to the recycling plant."

"At least it was being disposed of properly."

"Yes, but the hassle of it all. I mean people were just content with throwing it on the street, but now they have to collect it all and make sure it isn't thrown outside. Then they've got to bring them to recycling centers, or wait for the weekly collections. Not exactly a convenient arrangement. Come to think of it, people had just gotten used to the concept of throwing it outside and then complaining about how bad the state of garbage on the street is. No, what your government tried to do is change the way people think. And if making them ethically responsible wasn't going to work, the threat of eternal damnation just about sealed the deal."

The patient looks down on the table and his bound arms under the straight jacket while Dr. Faisal continues taking notes. Smiling at his patient, the doctor continues to engage him in conversation.

"I'm glad you're opening up to me. This is the right way to finally move on and realize just exactly what needs to be done. I mean this is sort of the thing that'll get things fixed."

"What things?"

"Well, all you've talked about. And of course, law and order."

The patient looks up and shows a face full of concern as his eyes stare wide at the doctor.

"What's wrong with law and order?"

"Nothing's wrong. Everything is working along swimmingly. Traffic moves along well, no one travels the wrong way on roads, street crime has just about ended. Even incidents of physical and sexual abuse are beginning to dwindle down."

"That's... good, isn't it?" The patient asks in wonder.

"It would be, were it not for the price everyone has to pay. Anyone who dares travel the wrong way on the road loses their vehicle and their license. Cars must now have at least four occupants inside in order to come out on the main roads. If you're traveling solo then it's a bicycle for you, or walking. And of course street crime is going to end if the criminal ends up getting shot in the head thanks to the newly privatized police force."

"The police departments were corrupt," the patient replies. "Every single officer was politicized in one way or the other. They were no longer loyal to the state."

"So instead they were all dismissed and contracts were given to private security firms to start policing the different cities. They were given all the equipment and training, but they all lacked a moral conscience. All they could see were targets. And not just literal targets they could kill but statistical targets."

"Like a business. They needed to show performance."

"That they did. They started policing every street corner, more private policemen than there were pedestrians. Arrests increased, penalties increased, shootouts of criminals increased."

"It made people safer."

"But who would account for their actions?" The doctor asked passionately. "Who would ensure they were killing actual criminals? Where were their trials? Where was the evidence? Due process?"

"Evidence?" The patient's voice shows a bit of emotion. "Ask the people they saved. Ask the people who are alive and have their possessions intact thanks to them."

"Sure, the social media is chock full of videos and testimonials about the people who were saved. But what about the families of the so-called offenders? At least before they could meet them in jail or help them with a legal defense. Now it's like any person suspected of criminal activity is to be killed on the spot."

Hearing this, the patient scowls.

"Let the punishment fit the crime."

"Hmmm," the doctor lets out a deep breath. "Interesting you point that out. Particularly how other offenders were treated. Suspected rapists would be castrated, suspected wife-beaters would be beaten up black and blue. Suspected acid attackers would have acid thrown in their eyes, while suspected gropers had their hands cut off. Suspected pedophiles would be stoned, and the suspected adulterers would have their heads sticking out of the sand till the vultures pecked them clean. Bit barbaric, not to mention extreme."

"I don't know what you're trying to say here, doctor." The patient says. "All of this was to make the kind of crimes they committed a thing of the past."

"I don't doubt the intentions, but the means? And these crimes aren't even being stopped by this private police force. That responsibility has been taken care of by the Youth Collective. Deputized youngsters who haven't even finished their education yet, who still need to develop their sense of empathy, are being tasked to mete out vengeful justice just like their private police counterparts. And that means even less accountability."

"People were saved."

"Not all of them. Not the guy whose wife faked an injury just to get him beat up. Not the student who maligned her university professor as a sexual predator. Not the housekeeper who accused her elderly employer of being a pervert. They just became headlines of this government's *achievements* in cracking down on crime."

"None of them were innocent!" The patient's tone is elevated again. "All of them were found guilty. If they weren't, they wouldn't have been noticed."

"Well, that's what you can keep telling yourself. But in reality, all your government has ever done is drive people against the wall. Curtailing civil liberties and legal rights just to ensure law and order is nothing short of totalitarianism."

"People need protecting," the patient tries to lean forward even more. "They need to understand their carefree lives come at a cost. And if they need to be controlled to ensure they live their lives happily, then it is a price they must be ready to pay. Only the guilty have been punished."

"Ah, I see we're getting to the root now," the doctor scribbles in the notepad.

"What do you mean?" The patient looks puzzled.

"I've always wondered how all these measures came about. Surely they could be discussed over meetings, or maybe just one person suggested them. So I have to ask if this is something you all came to a joint consensus about, or was it you on your own?"

"We all knew what was best for the people."

"Well yes, but as the Supreme Minister, you had the final say. And everyone would blindly follow whatever you said, even if it meant losing their freedom. They chose you because you could do something different than the previous corrupt leaders. They made you Supreme Minister because you captured their imaginations with a notion as simple as change. Well they got their change. *We* got our change. But was it for the better? Was it worth it?"

Taking all of this in, the patient, the Supreme Minister ponders and closes his eyes, till he opens them again with a face full of realization.

"Oh, I get it now. That's why I'm here. Because I tried to change things. Because I tried to fix what was wrong with society. Because the country was so used to the way things were they couldn't see the right thing for what it was. Instead, they thought I was mad to bring about such reforms. That's why I've been put here."

"Absolutely not!" The doctor smiles. "You're here because you needed to disappear. Terrorists tried to kill you and therefore you needed to be protected. People know you're safe, that's all that matters. In here, you're just an anonymous patient who needs psychiatric care. No one would even think of looking for you here. When the time is right, when the terrorist threat has been eradicated, you'll be brought back to lead the country again."

The Supreme Minister looks intently at Dr. Faisal and leans forward, a wide grin forming over his handsome, shabbily bearded face.

"There are no more terrorists. We got rid of them all."

The doctor smiles as well.

"Right. So you did. Well, I better go and order that behari boti then."

Dr. Faisal gets up, his chair grinding the tile floor as it slides backwards. As the doctor reaches for the doorknob, he looks back again at his patient.

"It has been a pleasure ... *speaking* with you, Supreme Minister."

The grin doesn't leave the Supreme Minister's face as the doctor exits the room.

KINDNESS

With another door slamming into his face, Zeeshan lets out a sigh of exasperation, not to mention exhaustion. He furiously crosses out the address from his clipboard as he puts back the sample bottle of toilet cleaner back in his kit bag.

Once he hoists the bag on his shoulders, he looks at the clipboard to see just how many more apartments he has to go through before the hour is up. The economy hasn't been kind to him after he was downsized from his previous company, and landing a new job has been difficult with the trend of hiring freezes all across the country. It's the only reason he took on this temporary gig of selling fast-moving consumer goods door to door, the new toilet cleaner proving to be difficult to sell.

"Guess people would rather be well fed than have a clean toilet."

Approaching the next door, he straightens his product-branded cap and works up a smile on his face. He'll need to make the best impression he can if he hopes to fulfill his quota for the week. Only ten more bottles to go to get the additional bonus, and with his ambitions, Zeeshan can use every rupee he can get.

He presses the button for the doorbell, one of those buzzer types that come standard with the apartment. His head shakes just enough to show he's nervous, and his foot is tapping in anticipation.

"Please don't make me do this."

Realizing he would need to make more of an effort, Zeeshan sheepishly knocks on the door for good measure and hopes he won't have to ring the bell again. He was always taught in school to ask at the door three times before leaving. He figures he can ring the bell and knock three times each for good measure.

Just then, the rattling inside relaxes his tense shoulders as he prepares for the next stage of the pitch. The door opens just enough for Zeeshan to notice there is a small chain holding it back. In the small black space between the door and the sill, he can make out a singular eye and a pair of lips looking towards him.

"Good afternoon. Are you the lady of the house?"

It takes a moment till he hears the nervous voice of a woman.

"Yes?"

"Hi! My name is Zeeshan and I hope I'm not disturbing you this fine afternoon. I just wanted to take a moment to tell you how the new Zappo toilet cleaning solution can change your lifestyle. Would you..."

Without warning, the door clicks shut, taking the wind out of Zeeshan's opening monologue.

"... like to hear more... *Terrific!*"

He lowers his head and turns around to leave before he can hear the unmistakable sound of the chain coming off and the door opening again. At once, the spring returns to his step and Zeeshan's smile lights up again as the lady of the house stands at the half open door.

"Toilet cleaner?" She asks timidly.

"Why, yes!" Zeeshan brings out all his confidence. "With the new Zappo range of toilet cleaning products, you can now have the shiniest and cleanest bathrooms and toilets, and rest assured you'll be protecting your loved ones from the threat of harmful diseases. If you don't mind, I could give you a full demonstration and preview of what our products can do."

"Ummm," she hesitates, "I don't know if it's a good time."

"It will hardly take ten minutes, and you'll be amazed with the results."

"Well, I guess..."

"Splendid! Mind if I come in?"

"Oh, okay."

Not looking a gift horse in the mouth, Zeeshan invites himself in carrying his kit bag along. As the woman shuts the door behind him, Zeeshan looks around at the average-looking living room with an L-shaped sofa and TV on the wall. There are a few picture frames of the woman with her husband and the odd knick knacks.

"Water?" She asks, trailing behind Zeeshan.

"Oh, thank you. That would be nice."

Zeeshan sets his bag down on the tiled floor and sits on the sofa, finally able to relax after a tough day. He is quite optimistic he can manage the final sale for the day *here* now that he's already inside. Plus the woman doesn't seem to be that hard to negotiate with. He wonders all this as she returns to hand him a glass of water.

"Thank you," he smiles as she takes a seat on the backless section of the L-sofa.

As he sips, he can't help but regard the woman with some concern as he tries to match her with the pictures of her on display. While all those snaps show a delightful, energetic and vibrant woman enjoying herself with her husband at scenic backgrounds of natural beauty, the woman sitting here - though undoubtedly the same person - looked much like a worn-out version of the woman in the photos.

"Um, are your children not home?" He asks.

"Oh, I don't... I don't have any."

"Oh, right. I'm sorry." Zeeshan answers sheepishly. "I hope you don't mind my mentioning it Ms., uh..."

"Zainab."

"Okay, well anyways. So like I was saying, Zappo has an amazing range of not just toilet cleaning products, but also other products that are ideal for all modern home cleaning needs. We provide an extensive range of toilet cleaners, surface cleaning liquids, kitchen cleaning liquids as well as cleaning accessories. Mops, plungers, toilet brushes, kitchen scrubbers; you name it. I have a complete catalog here that'll tell you of all the things you can obtain to get your house not just cleaner than clean, but also 101% germ-free. All our liquid products are guaranteed to wipe out 99.9% germs and cause absolutely no irritation to eyes or skin, or you get your money back."

"It is pretty impressive," Zainab interjects as she clasps and twiddles her fingers, "but I've been using Happy brand products for some time and..."

"And I'm sure you've developed a certain affinity for your brand. I can understand it's not easy to just change old habits so easily. But believe it or not, you get absolutely fantastic savings with Zappo if you act now. For instance, here's our big budget offer. You can buy thirty bottles for the price of fifteen. That's exactly half of what you would need to spend. And the results are outstanding to say the least."

"Thirty?" Zainab raises her eyebrows. "I only buy three a month for my bathrooms."

"Perfect! So you'll have ten months' worth of stock. I can also assure you the expiration date of all products is from the current month for a year, so you won't have to worry about that either."

"But still, that is a lot."

"Think of the savings, Ms. Zainab! Plus no need to go out every month to buy those with your groceries."

"Um, I don't know..."

"Well, all right. I see you would be apprehensive. So how about this: fifteen bottles for the price of ten. Five extra bottles!"

Zeeshan bends towards his bag and pulls out about five stacks of three bottles each, all of them emblazoned with the Zappo logo and pictures of a spotless white bathroom. He gently places them on the coffee table in front of them where he had put down his glass of water earlier.

"If basic blue isn't your kind of flavor, we also carry citrus orange or lemon, as well as breezy green. And if you act now..."

Zeeshan then pulls out a plastic packet of four small spherical tokens.

"... you get two packets of our brand new cistern blocks absolutely free, four in each packet. Simply drop them into your flush tank and be amazed. They clean, freshen and also help prevent lime scale,"

"This is all pretty overwhelming," Zainab tries to manage a smile.

"Trust me, Ms. Zainab, at these rates we're practically *giving* them away. Besides, we would like to see you become our customer for life. And we'll just be a call away if you need any more."

"But I'd have to... I mean what you say is all pretty good, but I've only heard about your company on TV. I don't know if this is right for me."

"I thought you'd never ask!" Zeeshan claps the cushion and picks up one loose bottle of Zappo toilet cleaner. "And that's exactly why we don't just say what we mean, we *do* what we mean! Which way is your master bedroom?"

"Um, that way," Zainab points without actually thinking it through.

"Brilliant!" Zeeshan cries out enthusiastically and charges off towards the direction of Zainab's finger.

"But wait, you can't just..."

"Now, now, Ms. Zainab," Zeeshan confidently assures her, "you are in for a treat as you get to see just how effective the Zappo range of products are."

"But you can't go in there," Zainab calls behind him timidly as she follows him. "I haven't cleaned up yet."

"Oh even better!" Zeeshan smiles, though it seems more like a grimace knowing he'll have to work a lot harder for this sale.

As Zeeshan disappears behind the bedroom door, Zainab slows her pace as she picks up her soft red heart-shaped key fob that also acts as her stress reliever. Her hand pumping the fob vigorously highlights the amount of stress she's under as she sheepishly walks inside the room. Her eyes face downwards as she can see the light coming from the bathroom door and the sound of liquid spilling.

Once she finally reaches the door frame, her breath quickens as she spots Zeeshan with his back to her and the bottle of cleaner spilling out its contents on the bare tile, splashing against his shoes. He finally turns around to face her with a horrified expression on his face, one that continues to become more and more fearful as he finally looks at her. She continues to breathe faster and pump on the stress ball even more as they both look towards the bathtub that used to be white, but is now caked dark-red both inside and out in both dried and wet blood. Even more distressing to watch is the collection of meat and skin inside the tub, and the remains of the upper half of a human skeleton next to the bathroom sink.

Zainab gulps as she watches Zeeshan turn around again, tears forming in his eyes out of fright and his hand finally letting go of the bottle. She knows that he wants to scream, his entire body is quivering, regurgitating in order to let out the terror that has bottled inside him. And he does, but not in the way she expects which relaxes her breathing now. She lets out a sigh of relief masked by the sound of Zeeshan throwing up in the toilet bowl.

*

Zeeshan shivers, he has been ever since he got back on the sofa in the living room. Sitting next to his bag that held the tools of his trade, he sits wide-eyed at the stacks of toilet cleaners he had put there earlier. A glass of water enters his field of vision as Zainab offers it to him, but he is too shocked to move. Either that or he is frightened of the woman who had timidly let him into a situation he wasn't at all prepared to handle.

"I'll just leave this here," Zainab says as she puts the glass down on the table in front of him.

"What... what have you done?" Zeeshan asks in a shaken voice, his earlier confidence and swagger depleted.

"He was a very nice person, you know," Zainab cracks a faint smile. "He was smart and funny and so caring in the beginning. But you know how it is. Good things don't last. We moved into a new house just for my sake, with his business he could afford it. But you can't run away from your past, can you? My mother in law comes to visit us once a week; she could never stand how we were making a life of our own."

"But, but why?"

"Last year I was pregnant. We didn't care much about what the gender would be. But she hounded him, filled his head with all sorts of things I never even thought of. She forced him to get the ultrasounds to find out what the gender was. And when it turned out to be a girl, she just went on the warpath. She did everything conceivable to turn him against the whole idea. She, *he...*"

Zeeshan gulps as he notices the tears forming around her eyes now. Even with all he's seen in the past half hour, his head tries to devote as much attention to Zainab's tale as he can.

"He was never violent before, you know. He wouldn't even hurt a fly. Or at least that's what I thought of him. He made sure I was provided for, given every kind of happiness I needed. But when it came to having a girl of my own, he just became a completely different person. It's as if a total stranger had put on his skin and pretended to be him."

The thought of skin jittered Zeeshan, though Zainab did not notice.

"What did he do?"

"You asked me if I had kids. I almost did. He, he... oh God!"

Confusion clouds Zeeshan's mind as he isn't aware of what to think of her now. Even if what she says is true, what he saw in the bathtub defies all reason and sanity.

"Look, I don't want to be any part of this!" Zeeshan finally manages to utter, reasserting himself just a little. "All I wanted to do was make a sale and go home. Ten more bottles and I could have gotten the extra commission. Fifteen would have been a cherry on top. But please, you don't have to buy the stuff. Just... just..."

"What?" Zainab raises an eyebrow.

"Just let me go. I promise I won't tell anyone about you or your..."

"Tell?" Zainab stands up abruptly looking incensed for the first time, something Zeeshan never imagined possible. "What do you think I am? I'm not a criminal or violent offender! He killed my child and continued his terror over me. I just did what anyone would do."

"Slaughter their husband? Cut them up into little pieces?"

"It was an accident. His violence was getting uncontrollable. I just picked up a vase and... I didn't know what I was doing."

Avoiding her body, Zeeshan carefully picks up the glass of water as he drinks it all in one gulp.

"So what now? He asks.

"I don't know," Zainab replies, dropping on the sofa with exhaustion. It's been two days that I've tried to get rid of his body. Everything I cut, there's more blood."

"Please, stop."

"And that was just his upper body. His ass and legs are in the other bathroom."

Zeeshan makes a huge effort not to hurl again.

"The whole house is a mess." She continues. "I'm sure there's blood everywhere and getting this cleaned up before his mother shows up is going to..."

In an instant, Zainab's expression changes as she notices the bottles of toilet cleaner.

"I'll take them all!"

"What?" Zeeshan stares at her flabbergasted.

"All fifteen bottles for the price of ten, right? I'll take them, and any scrubbing brushes you have."

"Oh *now* you want the cleaners?"

"I need them all to make sure this place is cleaner than clean, like you said. There shouldn't be a speck of blood in this whole house. I need the whole place cleaned up. And *you* can help me."

"You want me to help you clean up all the blood in your house and dispose of your husband's... remains?"

"I'm tired now, I've been at this for days. And you wouldn't have to touch the body parts. I'll put them in garbage bags and dump them around the city. You just help me clean up the house and the bathrooms, that's all."

"You must be out of your mind if you think I'll help you with this."

"Please, I'm desperate here. And you said you wanted to sell ten more bottles, right? Just help me with the cleanup and I'll take fifteen like you wanted, and then you can go home."

This sends a shiver up Zeeshan's spine for some reason, as he becomes a little more cautious towards her.

"What do you mean? You mean if I don't help you, you won't let me leave?"

"Oh come on!" Zainab sounds irate. "I am *not* a murderer!"

"Could have fooled me, lady!"

Zainab scoffs as she gets up again. She intently looks around her and then at Zeeshan, who doesn't know what to expect now before finally walking off towards the kitchen. She returns a few minutes later as Zeeshan remains sitting.

"You didn't run?" She asks.

"Uh..."

It hits him that he could have tried to run anytime he wanted to, and now regrets the decision. He then looks at her hands as it carries a tin container of cooking oil.

"Take it."

Curious and confused, Zeeshan takes the container which has the top cut open. It was quite common for these containers to be reused again for storing oil, but his eyes open wide when he removes the sheet of covering to reveal stacks and stacks of cash inside.

"There's close to a million in there, and I have another one just like this. He hid it where no one would think to look and I wouldn't dare to do anything with it. It's all *yours*, take it all.

"But, I couldn't..."

"Yes, you could!" She interrupts. "You look like a decent person, and certainly not someone who needs to be spending his days running around selling things door to door. Surely you must have something you want to do in your life."

Zeeshan's heart paces quickly as he fingers through the stacks of five thousand rupee bills inside the container, his mouth agape at the way things have been transpiring.

"A little startup of my own," he thinks out loud. "Maybe a little fast food restaurant."

"Good, that's good!" She exclaims. "Then don't think too much. Just help me and you can have the whole container."

Zeeshan looks at her face, her eyes pleading with desperation as they try their best to divert his attention from the bruises near them, and the dark circles underneath.

He looks at her face, which might have been full of life earlier, now driven towards despair and literally towards death. He wonders just what fate had befallen her, what had her husband done to push her over the edge. And then he thinks of the life she claims he had snuffed out in her womb.

He ponders all this, and then looks back at the cash-filled container as he puts it down to take out his cell phone. He swipes it a few times before dialing a number, which distresses Zainab as she feels he'll be alerting the police.

"Hello," Zeeshan calls out as the line connects. "This is Zeeshan. I've got a client here who'll need fifteen extra bottles. She's going for the thirty-for-fifteen deal. I'll text you the address. Oh and throw in some scrubbing brushes and garbage bags, will you? Get them out here *a.s.a.p.* Thanks."

Zeeshan cuts the call and looks at Zainab, whose weary face shows some sign of life if her smile is anything to go by.

"Lady, you're going to need *a lot* more than fifteen bottles. Let's get started."

<u>10</u>

BEACON

"Beautiful, isn't it?"

"What?" Axar Alee asks, turning around to notice the stranger

"Can't you see it?"

On a pedestrian bridge over a busy thoroughfare, Axar Alee had been standing and looking at the morning rush hour picking up. Wearing a disheveled but fashionably expensive semi-formal shirt, Axar never realized just when the stranger had come up next to him. On first impressions, he has nothing in common with the short bespectacled man with gelled-back hair and a brown leather briefcase he placed on the bridge. While his own clothes are no doubt of the finest quality and stitching, Axar can clearly recognize the stranger's tie and half-sleeved white shirt as items purchased in a flea market. The same could be said about the briefcase too.

"I'm not much of a fan of the sunrise, actually."

"Oh, not that," the short man replies, "well, not *just* that. Can't you see it?"

He gazes downwards away from the sunrise, and instead leads Axar to stare at the oncoming traffic heading towards the city.

"It's as if they're coming right out of the sunrise, whizzing past in all shapes and speeds, carrying people heading towards their destinations. People with no knowledge of what awaits them at the other end."

"Are you some kind of philosopher or something?"

"Hardly," the stranger smirks.

"Whatever! That's a pretty nice monologue. I'd clap for you if I could, but I'd rather I didn't draw any attention to myself.

"I'm surprised none of them have recognized you."

"What?" Axar reacts. "How do you..."

"I believe you're on TV all the time. Though I hardly ever get the time to watch anything you actually work in, I do get to spot you in your morning show every now and then. Axar Alee, isn't it? With an 'X' and two 'Es'. You always wear such exquisite shirts. Are you about to go to one now?"

"No, nothing that simple. You think I'd be standing here to go to a morning show?"

"Ah, I see." The stranger pondered, "So perhaps you're here to commit a grave mistake then."

Axar Alee looks at the stranger with muted disgust. This little man he just met knows more than he should. He's tempted to grab him by the collar to get some answers, but discretion would be the better part of valor.

"Whoever you are, you have no idea what I'm here to do."

"Probably not, but you can tell a lot about the way someone is standing over a bridge waiting for the traffic to pick up to get a fairly good idea of what he might do."

"Okay, fine! You know. So I guess you should walk away right now. Standing at the spot from where a man plummets to his death doesn't exactly sell you well as just a bystander."

"I'm sure it's none of my business..."

"Damn right it isn't!" Axar interjects.

"But don't you think taking your own life like this is just a tad too extreme? What could possibly be so bad to lead you to this?"

"What the hell do you care? You don't even know me."

"I know *of* you. I know there are people who love and admire you, though I personally don't think much of your target audience, no offence. But surely it's the adoration you crave."

Axar's rigid face seems to warm a little, as if undergoing a wave of emotions.

"It was all I ever wanted; to be a star. To be *someone!*"

"Well I'm certain there's more for you to do. More for you to live for."

On hearing this, Axar can barely contain his laughter.

"To *live* for?" he chuckles. "That's hilarious! If only you knew I have *nothing* to live for."

"I see. Well, is it the heart?"

"What?"

"That's what it typically is. Someone broke your heart and you can't live without her. Or maybe the morning show circuit isn't doing it for you anymore..."

"I'm *dying*, okay?!"

The stranger is taken aback. Axar seems satisfied, knowing this person wasn't at all expecting to hear this.

"Dying? You mean *now*?"

"Yes, and not just because of ...*this!*" Axar pulls at the guard rails with his hands. "I mean I'm literally dying."

Taking a deep breath, Axar closes his eyes wondering if he had said too much. But this stranger doesn't look like the kind of person who would be from the press. In fact, he looks and feels like someone Axar should trust, though he can't put his finger on exactly why. So now, he saw no reason to hold back.

"Before all of this, all the fame and glory... I was just Azhar Ali with no 'X' and no 'Es'. I was just a student who didn't like studying. Instead, I wanted to be in the limelight, to be a model. An actor, even! I wanted to get into that glamorous world. To have my face on every screen and to be adored by millions. Yeah, you're right; I craved the attention. And I would do anything to have that life."

Axar, or Azhar, takes a deep breath and stares back at the sea of vehicles coming his way.

"But that's the problem with wanting something: you're not the only one. And it wasn't easy at first; getting rejected or having to pay cash for the privilege of getting to be a bit player in some photo-shoot. That's when *he* came along and I got lucky."

"He?"

"Famous actor slash director slash producer slash media mogul. I'd rather not name names."

Azhar looks back at the stranger expecting him to pry, who just stared at him with the face of someone who genuinely cared. A bit of uncomfortable silence later, Azhar continues.

"He saw me at an audition and even though I didn't get in, he made it his business that I get under his wing. I was over the moon! To be loved by adoring fans was one thing, but to have such care and attention by someone who had legions upon legions in his thrall was something I never even imagined. He made sure I got what I wanted, got me into top billing for fashion shows and photo-shoots. Everything changed overnight."

"Sounds like he has been nothing but benevolent to you."

"You think so? I don't blame you. I've known him for years, and even when I look back at it now, it still feels like he genuinely cared for me and my success. But I was young. I didn't know any better. I had heard stories about people, rich and famous. Their indulgences, their vices... all just whispers by people who didn't make it big and washed out without even a second in the spotlight. I didn't think it was possible, least of all from someone like him."

"What happened?"

"There was a party, I forget when. Just a private gathering at a farmhouse somewhere outside the city. Lights, music, girls just ready to jump right at you without a care in the world. And then there was booze, followed by the drugs. It seemed like everything was in a spin, and at that moment I don't know how it happened. Maybe it was the booze or the drugs, or both, but *he* had me right where he wanted. He wanted the price for all he had done for me. He wanted *me*. And... How could I say no? I... I thought the world of him. He could have asked me to jump off a cliff and I would have. So when he, when he pushed me down on his bed, I... I..."

Azhar chokes while tears run down his cheeks.

"How could I say no?"

Even through the corners of his wetted eyes, Azhar could see the look on the strangers face. He couldn't really label it, but he knew what it was.

"If my father were still alive," Azhar finally speaks, "he'd be looking at me the same way you are now."

"It must have been difficult."

"That was just the start!" Azhar rubs the tears off his face. "I wasn't the only one. There were others, so many others who he did the same for, and the same to. And then there were the ones like him, the ones who exacted the same price for fame. Once it all started, it never stopped. This cycle kept going on for years, till eventually I hit it big with a few TV serials all thanks to him. Things quieted down after, though there were a few parties here and there, a few quiet meetings at hotels; men and women alike. But I had control. I would never do anything myself to the others. I tried to be different from him, to not abuse the position I had. But it's all irrelevant now."

"You said you were dying."

"It started months ago. At first it was fits and flu and the feeling of a jackhammer tearing away into my head. Then the rashes came and I had to get off the show for a bit. I didn't want to go to the proper doctors, so just painkillers and other over-the-counter drugs kept me going. I got a lot better and came back on the air. But just recently, it all came back, fiercer than ever. I had put off going to the doctor just so the press wouldn't hound me after my health and everything, but I had no choice. I went in secret and got tests done. I found out yesterday. The HIV had progressed into AIDS a lot quicker than anyone could have expected, but given the lifestyle I've had... I'm getting what I deserve."

"I'm sorry."

"Not as sorry as I am. Not as sorry as all the others who had their lives ruined by people like me."

"You mean people like him?"

"Who can tell the difference? I'm just as terrible and to blame."

"I don't think so." The stranger's voice now sounds more assertive than its previously casual tone. "I think if you were given the chance, you could certainly make amends."

"I doubt I could do anything to undo the damage I've done, both to myself and to the others."

"It's no longer about you, or even the limited number of people you were with. It goes far beyond, to people who made similar choices in their lives..."

"Mistakes. Like you said: grave mistakes."

"It's not for anyone to judge. You may believe it was a mistake now that you look back at it, but you didn't then. Neither did anyone else who had it even worse. Some didn't even have a choice if they were forced into it. Some did it for reasons both selfless and selfish. But maybe they won't have to endure it any more than they should. Maybe you can turn around what happened to you to bring some good out of it."

"How?"

"You should know; you're the *star*. Use your one asset that will change the way people think about all of this. Enlighten them of what happens behind closed doors and what some people are forced to do."

"No! That's ridiculous! Tell everyone my entire life, my career is all based on being someone's indulgence? That I had to bend over to win the prize? Do I look insane to you?"

"You're the one about to commit suicide. You tell me who's insane."

"Look," Azhar finally sounds determined, "you look like a reasonable person, so tell me just how is shouting out to the world about what happened to me and what I did going to change anything? Do you have any idea what would happen to me if I did?"

"You're the victim here."

"Based on what evidence?"

"Your word."

"Ha! That doesn't make anything better."

"Oh you can rest assured it'll get far, far worse. You will be ridiculed, ostracized from the people you know, the community you work for. Your friends and your family will want nothing to do with you, and you'll become a pariah in the eyes of the media. And of course, they might throw you in jail just for being a deviant."

"That's very comforting," Azhar scoffs.

"But imagine what the weight of your words would hold for people who need to hear them. People who aren't that different from you, people who have fallen victim to similar circumstances or worse. Imagine the connection you would make with them. Not only will you voice the grief and anguish they have suffered, but in you they will find a champion. The knight they have waited so long for. The ones who may be at death's door or the ones who couldn't carry on when they found themselves standing on a bridge just like this one."

"You think I'm stronger than them?"

"Personally, I don't have an opinion either way. You could go ahead and jump just like you planned to and I would be on my way to catch my bus just as I planned to.

You wouldn't be able to do much once you're dead though. People would wonder over what happened. Maybe you were depressed, maybe it was a streaming video gone wrong. There would be candlelight vigils and sad tweets, crying selfies and even those tribute montages the morning shows crave for."

He manages to look at Azhar for the first time, mostly from the corner of his eyes and spectacles.

"But then, it won't be just you who dies today. You'll be killing the hopes of so many people who need to see there is a light for them."

"A light they don't even know is there."

"Not unless you show it to them. What's the point of earning all this recognition if you can't even use it for good?"

"So you think I should be a martyr for this?"

"Every purpose in history has needed its fair share of martyrs. Without them, there would be no purpose."

"Still, no one would believe it. They'd believe I had AIDS sure enough, but no one would believe how I got it. And even if they could comprehend the events that happened, they'd find a way to put the blame on me; that it was my fault I wanted to get ahead in my career, or even how I kept quiet about it all this time. I'd just become a laughing stock."

Azhar now looks at the stranger, who stares back at the wave of vehicles still rushing by under them.

"Many great people throughout history had their share of hecklers, of people who laughed them into ridicule. And yet, no one remembers the people who laughed. But everyone remembers the people who were laughed at. *They* were the ones who changed the world. And so can you."

He then stares further ahead, all the way across the horizon.

"Or you could dive head first into one of those speeding minibuses, and see where it gets you."

Azhar looks ahead as well at the object that had the short man's attention. He realized there was not much else to be said, and no one else was going to decide for him. He had a choice now, which is more than he had when he stepped foot on the bridge. Much like the choice he had all those years ago when he put his career over his dignity, this feels like the toughest one he has ever faced. But unlike then, when he didn't calculate all the repercussions, this time his gut trembles at the prospect of the uphill battle awaiting him.

So for the first time in a long time, Azhar lets his gut decide what to do. He steps onto the middle rung of guard rail separating him from certain death while grabbing the top rail with both hands. He waits for the minibus to gain speed and snake its way past the other vehicles like all minibuses do without a care in the world. And for the first time in ages, he could hear his gut wrench inside of him.

Not once does Azhar look at the short man, nor does the stranger try to do anything as he stands motionless. Azhar takes a deep breath and closes his eyes, while the irritating sound of the minibuses' customized loud horns coupled with the bus conductor yelling out the various destinations approaches him. He puts his head down and waits as the sound of the minibus whizzes past, along with all the other vehicles in its wake. In all this time, Azhar's grip tightens on the guard rail.

Once the sounds have died down, Azhar finally exhales and loosens his grip as he steps down. After the whole experience, he couldn't help but laugh and cough at the same time. With deep, labored breaths, Azhar looks up at the stranger, who has a smile on his face.

"This was... I mean I don't know. I don't know how to thank you."

"Thank me?"

"Yeah!" Azhar replies with a burst of enthusiasm, relishing his new lease on life. "If you weren't here, now, in this very moment, I would just have gone through with it."

The short man looks at the tips of his shoes, his smile still present on his face.

"If I weren't here... now, at this very moment," he looks at Azhar one final time, "I would just be early for work."

And with that, he bends down to grab his briefcase from the bridge and turns around towards the exit stairs of the bridge, without even saying goodbye. Azhar tries to stop him, but couldn't as he watches him walk off into the crowd starting to gain behind him.

Azhar may never know who this man was, or what he was doing here, or why he decided to stop and talk to him, but he realizes things happen for a reason. His gut is still talking to him, just like it was when it told him that leaping off the bridge would be the easy way out. Whereas staying back to fight for the people who had been victims like him would be the really brave thing to do.

There is indeed an uphill battle waiting for him and the repercussions would be disastrous. But there was something the stranger had said about making a connection, one he has spent all these years building with his audience and the entertainment community. Surely that had to amount for something. Surely there were people out there who would listen to what he had to say and be empathetic.

And then there would be the ones he would accuse, the powerful ones who think they can get away with their indulgences. Their standing and reputation in the industry had protected them until now. They can still use it against him, and most likely would do things to hurt him. But he doesn't care, not after now.

Azhar pulls out his smartphone and swipes away the plethora of missed call alerts before dialing a number.

"It's me. Yeah I'm fine. Listen, call a press conference. I want to make an announcement."

He listens intently to the voice at the other end.

"Oh believe me; they'll want to wear what I have to say."

<u>11</u>

EXILE

Just an hour before the sun sets, the park is brimming with life as children of all ages play and mingle over the various rides and slides. Oblivious to the life moving about its merry dance, Thorne walks past the women seated on the benches gossiping away at the latest fashion fad, or some scrolling past whatever has their eyes glued to their smartphones. He grimaces and ponders over their choices in life, trying to comprehend why they would want to squander away these precious few moments over something so inconsequential.

He always wondered why they would never stop for a moment long enough to interact with the teeming beauty of nature all around them, at the small cats chasing each other or the dogs taking a shit in secluded spots of grass. He shakes his head at those who have consciously decided not to benefit from the walking track and breathe in the fresh air from the lush green trees nearby, considering the state of smog surrounding the rest of the city.

Wonders, till at last he arrives at a bench tucked away towards the children's play area, where a solitary woman sits and is engrossed in – much to Thorne's amusement – a book.

"Good evening, Mrs. Saif." Thorne speaks with a hoarse voice.

"Hello," Mrs. Saif looks up momentarily, squinting just a little. "Do I know you?"

"I hope so. We spoke a long time ago once."

"Really?" She wonders. "Sorry, but I don't forget faces, Mr. uhhh…"

"Thorne. Just Thorne. You may remember me from a trip we once took. The longest one of both our lives."

"Oh, from where exactly?"

"I think they call it Proxima here, but you know the name native to us, don't you?"

Mrs. Saif's eyes look a little curiously, till her brow settles and her face shows an indication of displeasure.

"I'm sorry. I don't know where that is. You must have me confused with someone else. Good day."

"*Papillon*. Very ironic."

"What?"

Thorne points at the object in her hands.

"Your book. About two prisoners trying to escape and failing over and over again. The irony is obvious, isn't it… *Ara*?"

On hearing her *real* name, Ara lowers and closes the book while sighing out of frustration.

"You'd better sit. You look strange standing over me like this."

"I was hoping you'd say that." Thorne smiles as he takes his place on the bench, keeping his distance from Ara.

"Why are you here, Thorne?" She asks out of frustration. "Why now, after all this time? I have nothing to offer you that'll help you in any way. I'm no longer the same person I was all those years ago. I have a family and children and a house and even a small investment in the stock market. My life is going along well."

"Don't you mean *plodding*? Look at you, Ara. You were something grandiose and powerful back then. Now you're just living the domestic dream of mommy blogs and bake sales and kitty parties. How the mighty have fallen, though in our case it's quite literally."

"I've come to peace with my circumstances. I've understood there's no way out for me, or for you either. And if you're here dredging up the past, it's obvious you still haven't been able to let go. Face facts Thorne: it's over."

"Nothing is over!" he sounds agitated, though he looks around taking care to ensure the public doesn't notice. "I still have more chances."

"Thorne," Ara rubs her forehead, "how long have we been here?"

"Far too long. Decades by my estimates. I've already survived the technological revolution. God, these people were so slow to move beyond analog computing. Did you know they had just invented the optical disk by the time I decided to intervene? Their growth was stilted and limited by their own capabilities and fear of failure. Just why we decided this planet was worth conquest is beyond me."

"We needed this planet, Thorne," Ara replies. "It has a vast supply of minerals and oceans. It's ideally suited position from its star made it a suitable habitat. Not to mention once our forces arrived here, we could have easily exploited all the other neighboring worlds. Gas and ice giants ripe for the taking and moons ideal for colonization. That's what our command had planned."

"As had *ours*." Thorne continued. "And considering our ongoing war, whoever of us set foot in this solar system first could have determined the outcome of the conflict between our two empires. Do you remember how we raced each other to get here? How we destroyed our ships en route?"

"Pluto, wasn't it? That's where we fought our final pitch battle. Our cruisers had depleted whatever energy they had and we couldn't let each other get ahead. So we destroyed our space cruisers and had to reach Earth using our own powers. Powers we lost upon arrival."

"Not to mention the technology we brought along," Thorne interjects. "So red was our hatred for each other, so intolerant were we of each other's kind that we couldn't fail our own peoples. So the moment we arrived on this backwater planet, we were left with nothing. Shells of our former selves with barely enough technology to establish our bases. All we could do was transform our appearances to the native humans and..."

"And create beacons to notify the home worlds of our arrival," Ara continues. "Yes, I could pick up your transmissions too. I tried my best to jam them while cannibalizing whatever crude scraps of technology this world had to offer, but you had figured out a workaround."

"So had you."

Both look away from each other as their reminiscing of past lives seems to have taken them to places they had forgotten the rest of their lives.

"I kept running the beacon, you know," Ara resumes. "Even after I got married, I hid the transponder in my husband's garage. I would do nothing but sit next to it whenever he left for work, checking the readings to see if there was any response. By the time my second child was born, I switched it off for good."

"Because you gave up!" Thorne sounds harsh. "You, the only one of your race here on this planet, from a world where war and conflict is second nature. Where your young are literally given birth amidst battle and must be weaned in the harshest of environments."

"I know," Ara rolls her eyes. "I was there."

"And you turned tame. The fight in you reduced to nothing more than getting your kids to eat their breakfast before getting them to school. You turned native and turned your back on your home world and your obligations to your empire."

"Right, as if you've done any better. Last I checked, you're still here."

"Yes, though not for a lack of trying. I continued to use my intelligence to find a way to get the empire here, or at least find a way back home. Even without my powers, I was smart enough to usher this planet into a new age. Pretty much all the scientific breakthroughs since we got here have been thanks to yours truly."

"The collider?" Ara inquires.

"That was probably the highlight, though I've gotten them far closer to quantum computing than they could have ever hoped for, certainly not for another half century. Even now, I've been travelling to China to get them to finally make their fusion energy project a reality."

"The artificial sun?" She ponders. "I had a feeling it would be you. Though I didn't even think you were still here, I realized humanity still had a long way to go. Your empire was always annoyingly intelligent for your own good. Winning wars and usurping planets based on your technological prowess rather than sheer warmongering."

"I'm just wondering what an alliance between our two empires would have been like."

"We would have torn each other apart," she grins. "Your people were so sanctimoniously smug. I mean, take you for instance. You claim to be a genius …"

"Correction," Thorne interrupts, "the geniuses on my home world called *me* a genius."

"And even then, you haven't been able to change much about your circumstances here on Earth."

"This isn't some army you can bully into shape, Ara. This is highly sensitive technology which these people hadn't even dreamt of before I came along. Their innate fears and selfish shortsightedness has kept them struggling and second-guessing everything they do. You have no idea just how hard it is to keep their artificial sun project together. Not just technologically, but also politically."

"Whatever your plans are Thorne," Ara speaks with her arms folded defensively, "are just that: yours. Why are you bothering me after all these years?"

"Because, I...." Thorne shakes his head as he mutters something under his breath.

"What was that?" Ara grins. "Didn't catch that."

"I... I need your help." Thorne answers sheepishly.

"Oh, that is precious!" she scoffs, trying her best to hold back her laughter.

"I'm here because I have no choice. You're the second smartest being on this planet, and I'll need your help to..."

"The answer is *no*," she says point blank.

"You haven't even heard what I have to say."

"I don't need to. And since you're *the smartest* being on this planet, you should have foreseen I wasn't going to help you."

"But why not?" Thorne sounds upset. "Don't you realize that without ever getting our signals, our home worlds must have thought we failed? That we encountered hostile threats on this planet, or in this system? Why do you think they never made a move to take this system? It's because our signals weren't strong enough to get our message across."

"And is that a bad thing?" She interjects. "You've been here as long as I have. Surely you must have seen how this world, these people..."

Ara takes a look around the park, directing Thorne's gaze all around the children and people entwined in the musical rhythm of their lives.

"... they don't deserve whatever we would have wrought upon them."

Thorne takes a deep breath as he closes his eyes in disgust.

"I can't believe you're saying this. You of all people. You, who could slaughter this entire country's population in no time at all. You, who once had powers to bend time to your will, to make their deaths as agonizingly long as possible, and repeat it over and over again. I just don't believe it."

"I'm sorry, Thorne. I really am. But I don't wish this world any harm. Because this is my home now..."

"This is not your home!" he sounds absolutely agitated, gaining some curious glances from the other women around the park. "Not to you, and certainly not to me. We don't belong here!"

"Yes, we do! Home isn't where you come from, Thorne. It's what you build, what brings you comfort, joy, love. I've found my home here, with the ones I love."

"Well, that is where we differ. You think this is love? Putting all these people at risk while you pretend to be one of them *isn't* love. I mean, I don't care either way for these beings... they pollute and kill and rape and main with impunity in their own world. They don't deserve you and certainly not me."

"But you've made their lives better, Thorne. Even if you don't care to admit it..."

"Stop, stop right there! Don't try to paint me out as some kind of savior. I'm not the hero of this story, and neither are you."

"I can't, Thorne. I just can't. Please, just go."

Ara turns her face away from the man sitting on the other end of the bench. And Thorne's expression now changes into something different, transitioning from disappointment to perhaps regret. Till it reaches one he can feel comfortable with.

Pity.

"You know, I actually feel sorry. For you. For all of these people. And for what I'm about to do"

Ara turns to look at him again, a little confused.

"What do you mean?"

"It would have been so simple, Ara. All you had to do was abandon everything here, come with me and we could have figured everything out. But you decided you'd rather be stuck here with your dose of domestic mediocrity. Well, if I can't have what I want..."

Thorne puts his hand inside his coat pocket, and pulls out a cobbled together cylindrical device.

"... then neither can you."

"Is that..." Ara's eyes squint and her face becomes horrified at the thought. "Is that an atomic disruptor?"

"As close as I could come to one considering my circumstances. But rest assured, it is fully functional and quite lethal."

With that, Thorne gets up from the bench and walks purposefully towards the children. Towards *her* children.

"Thorne, no! Stop!" Ara gives chase after him.

"There's one thing you said that makes some sense to me," he speaks without stopping or turning around. "Home is what you build, what you create. Well, since you've deemed it fit to deprive me of my home, it's only fair I take away yours."

He finally turns around to face her, his hand holding the atomic disruptor pointed towards her children.

"Please, no!" Ara pleads as her eyes fill with tears, much to Thorne's amusement.

"You know what? I've changed my mind. I'm actually *not* sorry anymore."

With that, Thorne pushes the button on the device which sends a particle beam towards the children, disintegrating their constituent atoms to nothingness to the horror of all the people and children present. It's as if the children weren't even there.

Ara can't believe what she has just witnessed, as her legs give out from under her. Thorne lowers the device while feeling an odd bit of satisfaction as he walks towards her as she is on her knees, her sobbing face in her hands while the public around them scrambles to get their children away.

"You killed them... I begged you not to, but you still killed them."

"I needed to, Ara," Thorne replies. "I needed to set you free from your little delusion. These people were all dead anyway. In fact, had things gone our way, none of them would even exist the way you know them now."

"You had no right to take them from me!"

"Correction. You had no right to them in the first place. You're an outsider. An exile. You formed and built foundations on sand, not caring none of them would ever last."

Ara's sobs continue to intensify as Thorne shakes his head.

"It's okay, Ara. It's alright. Sooner or later, you'll realize I was right. Sooner or later, you'll understand what the right thing is. And when that happens, I'll be right there for you. Perhaps sooo...ooo..ooo...

Thorne's mind can register his speech slowing and degrading, he can comprehend something is amiss with the present, till he feels himself walking backwards to the spot. The corners of his eyes can register the parents un-picking their children away from the play area and he can feel his arm lifting the device back up. His eyes turn again, his mouth stands agape as he notices the particle beam returning to the disruptor, while Ara's children return back to their constituent forms. It's as if they had never even left.

"What... what is this?"

Before he can fully piece it all together, a blinding white light surrounds the children as they disappear. Another surrounds the remaining children and another the parents and public in the park, all of them disappearing as soon as the flash of light subsides, blurring Thorne's vision a little. Once the haze clears, he can see himself surrounded by empty grassland and slides, swings and bicycles. Even the cats and dogs are gone.

It's just him. And Ara, as she stands in front of him.

"What... what just happened?" Thorne exclaims at last as he sees her in front of him.

"*Tsk.* Smartest man in the world," Ara smiles faintly, her tears still covering her face.

She then sets her hand on his coat and another flash of light blinds Thorne. Once his vision clears again, he finds himself desperate for breath and surrounded by perpetual darkness. A void only glittering with pricks of light surrounds him and a blazing heat pulsates behind him."

"Where... where are we?"

"The end, for you." Ara replies, hovering in the void in front of him.

"What do you mean?"

"You wanted to build an artificial sun? Maybe this'll help inspire you."

Thorne instinctively turns around, his eyes finally beholding the majestic and raging ball of eternal flame that was the center of this entire solar system, its infinite gravity pulling him towards it with a force unparalleled to anything he could imagine.

"No, this is impossible!" he tries to speak with only a scarce amount of oxygen. "We can't be here... you can't..."

His mind finally begins to see.

"Oh, you *bitch*! You absolute bitch! You got *your* powers back! No wait, you never lost them? They were just dormant until..."

"None of this is relevant, certainly not for the limited amount of oxygen my little bubble of air is giving you."

"Time reversal, teleportation, space projection... you had all the power you ever needed to leave the planet. You could have left anytime you wanted, and you could have brought your armies here to take over. But instead, you..."

"That's right. I stayed. I built something for myself. I built a family, I learned to love. And it's worth more than anything I had ever had before. Certainly more than raining hell on this world and exploiting the celestial wonders of this system."

"You gave it all up. Gave up your right to glory... for..."

"I did. And I'd do it all over again. Which, given my powers, I actually can. And I can certainly protect my home from the likes of you."

Ara hovers closer to Thorne, who seems to be running out of air and is barely hanging by a thread in the immense force of the sun.

"The question now is... what to *do* with you?"

"You're going to... you're going to let me fall into the sun, aren't you?"

Ara doesn't answer.

"You're..." Thorne begins to choke as his reserves of oxygen begin to fade, "... you're going to cut the last remaining tether to your old life. Once I'm gone, you're completely... truly all by yourself. No way for you to go back. No way to..."

"I know. It all ends once you do."

"You can't.... you can't do this..."

"Can't I? You're the genius. You claim I've gone native. That the fire in me is dead. That I'm no longer capable of the barbarity my race is known for."

Ara grabs his coat collar, his breath fading fast.

"Well then tell me, smartest being in this solar system: which is it? Give me a good answer, Thorne. Your existence depends on what you're going to say next. Tell me I'm a good person for letting you live despite you actually killing my children in front of my eyes. Tell me I'm not scarred enough just because my kids weren't in real danger. Tell me I should spare you because I undid my world falling apart thanks to you."

Her hand can feel the octo-valve heart inside his chest beating like a set of banging drums.

"Tell me I should care whether you live or die. Tell me that I'm the *hero* of this story."

Despite the coldness of space but perhaps due the blazing yellow star behind him, Thorne can feel himself sweat as his eyes begin to blink out of existence, as his supreme intellect is working overdrive to think of a good answer. All he can see is the supreme fury of Ara hovering in front of him, waiting.

Waiting.

12

DEFIANCE

The buzzer sounds exactly when the ding of Amna's smartphone alerts her that her latest social media update is up. She catches the assistant motioning her head and promptly gets up from the sofa in the outer office to make her way towards the chambers of the Associate Dean. Before entering, she takes in a deep breath and adjusts her hair enough to have the last bit of assertiveness in her.

Walking into the office, she notices the Associate Dean sitting comfortably at her desk, typing while examining the contents of her screen closely through her half-moon spectacles.

"Madam Zehra?" Amna calls as she stands next to a chair across from her.

"Sit." Zehra replies without looking away from the screen.

Amna sits down, rolling her eyes as she places her clutch on the desk. She swipes away at her smartphone, taking the hint that Madam Zehra would let her know when she required her attention. She continues to review her news feed and smiles as she taps away comments on the screen. The phone dings and she smiles again.

"Please put that on silent."

Amna does, and puts the phone on the desk too. She understands that Zehra is ready for her now. Nevertheless, Amna is all ready for her too.

"A legal notice," Zehra picks up a bunch of papers from her desk and pushes them towards Amna, "requesting the immediate termination of Mr. Sultan Babur from his teaching position at the university, a few affidavits of sworn statements given by two students who claim Mr. Babur made untoward advances at them, an entire social media campaign to oust him and the previously accused at this and other educational institutions under the *#NoMore* banner. And even a t-shirt."

"That was my idea," Amna replies confidently.

"I hope you're pretty pleased with yourself."

"Pleased?" Amna scoffs. "If the administration and the committee did their jobs right, there wouldn't be the need for protests like this."

"Ah yes, your sit-in at the campus grounds. That's today, isn't it?"

"Starts right after noon. You've got maybe three hours to do the right thing."

"And what exactly is the right thing?" Zehra asks, eyebrow upturned.

"Please don't make me spell it out for you, ma'am. We want the inquiry restarted and this time we want independent outside investigators. We want all the interviews done again and all the evidence closely re-examined."

"The only evidence we have is a paper that got a B+. Everyone on the faculty has re-examined it. It's an A- at best."

"And the comments. *Apply Yourself.* What do you think that means?"

"Well, call me old-fashioned, but it's what teachers write when they want their students to do more than..."

"That's right!" Amna interrupts. "*Do more.* The kind of euphemisms that have landed the previous teachers under hot waters. We all know how these shameless faculty members want students to *apply* themselves. That's made abundantly clear when they visit them in their chambers."

"Those matters are still under investigation," Zehra replies sternly, "and thus can't be commented on. But Mr. Babur's matter was concluded and the investigation exonerated him from any wrongdoing."

"Respectfully ma'am Zehra," Amna leans forward, folding her arms, "but we categorically reject the findings of your inquiry."

"The inquiry team was constituted based on faculty members recommended by the student council."

"Yeah well that was before we realized you all just looked out for yourselves. No, we want independent investigators in on this, or we take this to court."

"Funny, you know. Mr. Babur asked us to do the same thing. When the students persisted in shaming him on social media, he sent us a letter asking us to reopen the inquiry, get in outside investigators."

"Wow, what a sick joke! Apparently vermin have a sick sense of humor."

"Mind your tongue!"

"Apologies. Apparently *faculty members* have a sick sense of humor."

Zehra clasps her fingers and shakes her head.

"I expected better of you, Amna. You're one of the best and brightest, and you've got a splendid future ahead of you. I'll even give you due credit for effectively running such a valid social justice campaign. But look at what it has done to you."

"Done to me? Let me ask you this, *ma'am*; what has happened to you? You were one of the most steadfast role models for every single girl who stepped foot in this campus when you were teaching here. And after you broke the glass ceiling to become an Associate Dean, we could call you our mentor and role model proudly. You did something no one in this university's history had done, and you were the one who inspired us to take on the injustices. When eve-teasing got out of control, you were the one who pushed us to take a stand. You just about convinced us to take up batons and pepper sprays to start hitting back at sexually frustrated boys all around us."

"What is your point?"

"And now, when teachers, when custodians of students are showing themselves as perverts, trying to gratify themselves while holding hostage the future of bright young students, you lose all your teeth. Whatever happened to you, ma'am?"

"I have no issues with what you're trying to achieve, Amna. I've even supported you when it comes to pursuing harassment cases against faculty members."

"Oh really? Like hell! You've shown your allegiances clear enough. You're a university mouthpiece first and woman second."

"You do realize my responsibility is to the university as well. I have to be impartial."

"Why don't you just go ahead and say they've bought your silence?"

"Would you believe it if I said it out loud?" Zehra smirks. "You're pretty convinced every single word I say is a lie."

Amna sinks in her chair a little, as even she realizes she's pushing Zehra towards her breaking point.

"Okay look, I'll admit you have your limitations. And yeah, you're not on trial here. But then why are you defending someone like this monster. Two students have come forward. How many more need to be subjected to his kind of perversion?"

"Two girls with a vendetta who say he made untoward advances. Both of them who coincidentally happen to be friends with some of the other girls who reported the same advances against other teachers."

"See? Isn't that persecution? He must have been friends with those other teachers, and there is enough proof available against them. Text conversations, audio recordings, what more do you want?"

"Against the other teachers, yes. And those are under investigation. But nothing against Mr. Babur."

"Only a matter of time before proof comes out against him too."

"Like the faked and doctored text screenshots?"

Amna closes her eyes.

"Fine, *that* I know was an oversight."

"I saw your update about it," Zehra smiles. "You were just about to put your weight behind that third girl when it was revealed all it took was basic photo editing to create those images. Sloppy one at that."

"We distanced ourselves from that student. And you suspended her, too. Probably the only instance when the university took some expedient action."

"Right. That's very understandable."

"Well then understand this," Amna hits back. "We're going to keep on fighting. We already are against the other teachers. And *Mister* Babur is going to get what's coming to him. He's a liar and a pervert. He has used his position to elicit unethical favors from his students; he stares and ogles at girls in his classes, undressing them with their eyes."

"Excuse me?" Zehra's tone grows stern.

"Haven't you been keeping up with the updates online? Aside from the two girls who made their statements, other girls have been making statements online about the way he looks at them."

"The way he *looks* at them?" Zehra muses.

"What do you think he's doing there? His intentions have been made quite clear and show he's just like the rest."

"I've read the statements. The girls have mentioned it, but there's no proof."

"What do you need? Videos, pictures? I'll bet if you let that man into the classrooms, we'll be sure to get it for you."

"Did you know he had a daughter? One he loved more than anything in the world?"

"I bet he did!" Amna sniggers with disgust.

"She died recently when she was ten. Leukemia."

Amna's face recoils at the thought, her disgust transforming into shock and a latent kind of sympathy.

"Well, I'm sorry about that. I didn't know."

"That's right. You didn't. What you also didn't know is he watched her wither away in her body as her face once full of life disintegrated in front of his eyes. The university offered him a great healthcare coverage but he was away for a year tending to this matter. It wasn't because he was suspended due to the investigation. He just couldn't bear the fingers being pointed at him and having to grieve at the same time."

"You're saying he wasn't suspended after what those girls said about him? He stared at her all the time, and others have come forward saying the same thing. He was a pervert, and I'm sorry about what happened to him but..."

"You still don't get it, do you?" Zehra scoffs as she leans back in her chair, rubbing her temples.

"Get what?"

"You all thought he was ogling you, undressing you with his eyes and that made him an easy target for you to pick on. But the truth is he saw *her* in all of you. He tried to find his little girl in every single girl he taught. He tried his best to make sure you all would be the best you could be, just because of the life you had been blessed with. A life all of you squander with your ridiculous obsessions with being noticed or trendy or being a part of the latest fad."

Zehra leans forward towards the desk now, staring dead-eyed at Amna.

"So if you think he was being too hard on you and giving you challenging and uphill tasks, it was only because he wanted you all to apply yourselves and be more than just what you appeared to be. He wanted you to take advantage of the privilege you had of being in this institution so that you could do the very best. He was just doing his *job*."

"Oh yeah?" Amna scoffs and folds her arms. "Tell that to the poor girls who have come forward against him and claimed he wouldn't give them better scores. Tell that to the tormented students who figured it would take a lot more for them to satisfy his insane standards. In fact, I'd like him to man up and face the ones he's put through so much stress..."

"Mr. Babur committed *suicide* earlier today."

Amna's spiel is stopped dead in its tracks as Zehra's revelation leaves her speechless, knocking the wind right out of her.

"He left a note in his pocket when his body was found. His family had ostracized him and his community began pointing fingers. They were just about ready to drive him out of his apartment. Guess he decided he wasn't going to leave there while he was alive."

"But... why?"

"Because you managed to destroy the one good man this university ever had. You tarnished the reputation of a teacher so badly that he saw no other recourse but to let himself be judged in the hereafter. And what's even worse is because he was the one who gave his life, he also inadvertently provided a lifeline to any teachers here who may *actually* be perverts and harassers."

Zehra gets up from her seat and walks over next to Amna, who swivels to face her as the truth begins to register on her face.

"That's right. Your little movement you had launched against people who, for all I know should actually be taught a lesson for being horrible people, just shot itself in the foot. In the midst of chasing after actual fiends, you decided it would be okay to target anyone with a penis who rubbed you the wrong way, no pun intended."

"It..." Amna is at a loss for words, "it doesn't change anything. He probably committed suicide because he couldn't stand the shame of what he'd done..."

Zehra sighs, taking off her spectacles and putting them on the desk.

"Sure. That would be it. Whatever makes you sleep at night. Incredible how fast your mind works at jumping to conclusions. So a teacher tells you to apply yourself some more and you automatically assume it's assault. But you see, this is where you've bitten off more than you can chew. You've created an unprecedented situation even you couldn't have foreseen."

Zehra folds her arms as she watches Amna writhing, trying to get her bearings back as she breathes heavily.

"So understand this," Zehra continues, "the university board is going to issue a statement. We're going to announce he committed suicide. We're going to circulate the suicide note and also our findings that there was no evidence against him."

"No, you can't do that. You can't..."

"Can't what?" Zehra smirks. "Can't release the truth? Isn't this what you've always been begging for; for the university to be transparent? Well that's *exactly* what we'll be doing today. Mind you, we won't be mentioning your little witch-hunt or sit-in too much. Don't want to steal all your thunder. But once we're done, we won't be able to hold back the wolves. The faculty's union is going to come after all of you, and with the wave of sympathy they'll be on, there will not be a single genuine harassment case that'll get the attention it duly deserves. Why? Because one of your poor tormented souls couldn't stand getting a B+ in her paper."

Amna looks horrified as she looks around the room with shifting eyes, while Zehra burns a hole through her with her eyes.

"I hope you're satisfied with what you've achieved. You've given your opposition the one thing they never had: a *martyr*. It's more than you'll ever have. Unless of course you can stage some more protests or get some of your victims to commit suicide, you're left with very little options here."

Zehra turns around and heads back to her seat, not looking at Amna's shrinking frame anymore.

"Now please get out of my office. I have a statement to prepare. Hashtag that, why don't you."

Amna's bloodshot eyes look back at Zehra, who sits back at her desk and resumes working on the laptop. With nothing left to say, Amna gets up holding on to her clutch and smartphone as she heads for the door, her grip around the phone tightening for dear life.

"We won't stop, you know." Amna finally speaks, her voice cracking in her throat. "We won't stop the fight."

Zehra takes a deep breath while pausing her fingers over the keyboard.

"I hope so, for all our sakes I hope better sense prevails."

As Zehra resumes typing again, Amna finally opens the door, the tears unable to cease from flowing down her face but her head held up high.

<u>13</u>

AFTERTHOUGHT

Waking up to the cool and soothing sunlight coming in from the window, Ilsa stretches her arms as she removes the duvet cover, not minding the chill of a December morning. She has a smile on her face as her eyes open slowly, sitting up and placing a hand beside her. Feeling nothing but an empty space on the bed next to her, the smile disappears as she looks around her to eventually find her phone under the pillow. Her eyes pop out of their sleep-filled haze once she notices the time.

"Shit!"

Getting up and putting her flip-flops on, Ilsa puts on her robe and straightens her hair in the mirror, carefully removing some of the glitter near her eyes from last night. As she makes her way to the door, she notices her elegant and rich red wedding dress neatly hanging on the wardrobe door. Ilsa can't help but take a deep breath pondering over the whirlwind of events from her wedding last night, when she finally tied the knot with the man she most admired and had pledged to devote her entire life to.

And she starts off this wonderful journey by oversleeping on her first morning.

Rushing down the stairs and hoping he hadn't left yet, Ilsa tries to navigate around the lounge to find the kitchen entrance. She's only been here a couple of times but naturally it would take some getting used to. After shutting the door to the storage closet, she finally arrives at the bright and sunny kitchen only to be disappointed that her new husband is not there.

Instead, much to her chagrin, Andaleeb awaits her on the small, round dining table.

"It's 9:34."

Ilsa closes her eyes and takes a deep breath, knowing she's screwed up. And now, she has to contend with Andaleeb.

"His reporting time is nine in the morning. That means he needs to leave by eight to beat the traffic. And that doesn't even count getting the kids to school before that."

Opening and rubbing her eyes, Ilsa knows she can't answer back to Andaleeb just yet, no matter how much her voice stings.

"You're lucky they're at their grandparents'. Guess they figured you and Rohail should have the first night to yourselves."

Looking directly at the dining table now, Ilsa seems to have gotten enough confidence to finally give Andaleeb a response.

"I'll make the tea," Ilsa says. "Would you like some?"

"I'll have what you're having," Andaleeb grins.

Ilsa finds the kettle and puts some water in before setting it on the stove. She then begins to look for the tea jar in the cabinets one by one.

"Second one to the right." Andaleeb interjects. "Milk cartons are in the bottom cabinet under it."

"Thanks."

Obtaining the required ingredients from the spots Andaleeb mentioned, Ilsa adds the tea and milk to the boiling kettle. Looking over the stove, she knows she can't stand there for long and so she sheepishly makes her way to the dining table, taking a seat across from Andaleeb.

"Had a good night's sleep?"

Ilsa smiles as she thinks back to before she had surrendered herself to slumber.

"Eventually, yeah. Rohail and I, we uh... that is..."

Ilsa can't believe she's said all this, especially in front of Andaleeb, who just looks with the same stone-faced indifference as before. As she tries to control her blushing, Ilsa clears her throat and continues.

"Rohail is uh... very passionate."

"Yeah, I bet he is. You weren't too bad yourself."

"What?" Ilsa looks alarmed. "You could hear us?"

Andaleeb doesn't respond, merely raises an eyebrow.

"Oh right," Ilsa says. "Of course you could."

"As if I were right there."

"Kind of invasive, isn't it?" Ilsa ponders.

"Invasive?" Andaleeb retorts and smirks. "You're forgetting who Rohail was married to before you came along. Sure you're younger and smart and... and yeah I'll admit you're pretty attractive. But there's nothing you can give him that I already haven't."

"Hmmm, yeah sure," Ilsa smirks this time.

"What's that supposed to mean?" Andaleeb looks alarmed now.

"Oh, right." Ilsa's smirk seems to widen. "I guess you don't know we used to talk before the wedding. Of the things you two did and those you uh... didn't *let* him do."

It's Andaleeb's face that seems to get red now, only it isn't because it's blushing.

"Now who's being invasive?"

Ilsa feels a little bad for having brought it up, and regrets the direction this conversation seems to be heading. Without saying anything, she gets up towards the stove and gets two mugs out of the rack, rinsing them in water. She then pours the tea in the mugs and sets them on the table before sitting back down.

"I'm glad he found you though," Andaleeb speaks while looking at her mug. "For what it's worth, I'm glad you brought a smile back to his face. Especially after the last few months."

Ilsa sips her tea and looks at Andaleeb strangely, doubting her sincerity.

"I'm very happy to have met him. He brought out some happiness in me, too. I guess we both needed to meet each other. And I don't doubt he loved you incredibly. I hope I can get that too."

"Oh I don't doubt that at all. I could see it in his eyes yesterday all through the wedding. I could feel it in his voice while he spoke to you. The way he held your hand, the enthusiasm during the photo-shoot. It's as if he had rediscovered what it meant to love again. And that is why I'm both happy for him, and disappointed in myself."

"Why would you say something like that? You know that he..."

"Yeah, *yeah*, he loved me immensely too. But what had I done with his love? I let it slip from my grasp, gave all my time to the welfare of the kids and brought them up. He wasn't even ready to have children for a few years after our wedding, but I pushed him. And though he never complained after, I could see he was losing interest in our bond. But that's not his fault. I had lost interest in it way back."

"You were being a mother for his children." Ilsa retorted. "Regardless of anything, he knew it would happen."

"Doesn't matter. I could still have been more accommodating towards him. I could still have looked like I didn't have a dark cloud hovering over my head. But my affection for him had transformed into care and attention for the kids. And he could see that. I'm surprised he didn't go out and find someone to cheat on me with."

Ilsa continues to sip the tea, obviously distraught at what she's hearing. She doesn't know how to respond but doesn't need to as Andaleeb has a lot more to say at the moment.

"But just being with you has made him regain his smile. Like friends meeting after ages, or a prisoner coming out back into the world, he has found the excitement in his life. Your youth has invigorated him in ways I never could, not that I tried in the last few years. But who knows. Maybe once you start looking after the kids, you might lose that new-wife shine too."

Ilsa has both her eyebrows raised now, as if something had just hit her. That doesn't stop Andaleeb from carrying on, actually looking forward to the remaining diatribe.

"Oh, that's right. You're going to be the new *mommy* too, right? A one-stop solution for all of Rohail's problems. Taking care of the kids, helping them with their studies. I hope you're good at Math. Babur is in grade five now and Algebra is quite the undertaking. And Zoha? She's still little, but she's going to need something more creative if you're going to make a place in her heart. All of that while keeping Rohail happy and feeling young and good again. I don't envy you right now... well, aside from envying you for being my replacement."

Ilsa sets her mug down with some force, making it audible enough to echo around the kitchen and obvious enough for Andaleeb to realize she's pushing too far.

"Guess I hit a nerve there," Andaleeb smirks again.

"Fine, I *get* it!" Ilsa finally speaks. "You've been the dedicated and perfect mom and wife, and been able to manage both your roles reasonably well. But I'm guessing you didn't go to some finishing school or take a course on being a domestic mastermind..."

"I have a Bachelor's degree in Home Economics, actually." Andaleeb can't help but interject.

"Well, *hurray* for you!" Ilsa retorts. "But let's face it; nothing can prepare you for what's really needed, for doing what needs to be done. Any job, any occupation, all that training can get you in the door but the rest is all on you. The day you had entered this house and Rohail's life, you must have been terrified. You probably didn't know what to do or what to expect out of him. Be it love or arranged marriages, people are never what they're like before the Nikah is solemnized. You must have frozen the first time you were told to make the tea or cook the food. You must have been scared to death the first night he sat next to you on the bed. And you must have just cowered so many times when you went to the delivery room."

"Really? Are we *really* having this conversation?"

"But even if you did, it's okay. There's no shame in being afraid of doing something new. It's what makes us human."

"Right, and you would know about that, wouldn't you? I mean, at least I'd been preparing for being a wife my entire life while you did your Master's in what, marketing? You gave up a good and comfortable job plus all your career ambitions just so you could devote yourself to my husband and children. You must have been terrified too, and so you cut yourself from your entire existence just so you could be a good mother and partner."

Ilsa waits for Andaleeb to continue, but is surprised at the silence.

"Was that supposed to hurt me?" Ilsa finally inquires.

"Actually, yeah. But now that I say it out loud, I think I can empathize with you. Look at me, trying to bring you down just because Rohail wants to move on with his life. It's not your fault I stopped loving him the way he wanted, or that we drifted apart. I guess it's true these stupid soap operas do nothing but pit women against each other."

"And it's not your fault either," Ilsa tries to sound reassuring. "Rohail could have been more understanding of what you were going through. You were doing what was best for everyone, including the kids. And it certainly isn't your fault that you..."

Ilsa stops abruptly, realizing the next few words to come out of her mouth would no doubt set Andaleeb off. That still doesn't stop Andaleeb from knowing it already as she looks at Ilsa with a subdued fury.

"What, not my fault that I got *cancer*? Not my fault that I couldn't do more for my family even if I wanted to? Not my fault that I left no choice for Rohail but to find a replacement? What is it if not my fault?"

"Your cancer is not your fault, Andaleeb. Why would you even think that?"

"I don't know! Maybe because I wouldn't be more amorous to my husband? Maybe because I'm some shrew who keeps taking the fun out of things just so my kids can have a great future? Maybe because I've yelled and scolded them, made them cry for taking away their tablets and video games just so they could eat their food without being zombies for twenty minutes? Is that my reward for being a responsible spouse and parent? A terminally life-threatening disease?"

Andaleeb's barrage of questions has no doubt unsettled the new bride and Ilsa is overwhelmed by the emotional onslaught. She has absolutely no answers that could even begin to heal Andaleeb's fractured soul and anything she said now might just make things worse. Which is why she's almost grateful Andaleeb hasn't finished just yet.

"No, I don't expect you to give me answers. I mean you weren't even part of our lives till after I got my final prognosis. That's when everyone kept telling Rohail's parents and they started filling his head with ideas for finding someone else. Who's going to take care of the kids, they said. Who's going to keep your son happy, they said. Like I was some kind of electronic appliance you could just replace after it had finished its life expectancy. Just your luck you came into his notice."

"It's going to be okay," Ilsa sounds somber. "We can figure this out. I don't have to be alone. You can be with me to guide me through."

"Well, that's one benefit of this ridiculous piece of *technology*." Andaleeb smiles. "I mean, leave it to men to come up with this stupid piece of tech that allows dead people to leave their memories and thoughts in some artificial intelligence chip before they die, so that their grieving loved ones can have them *implanted* in their own heads. Leave it to women to create a law that makes it mandatory for all husbands to get their previous wives' memories implanted in the new wives, so that *both* his wives could be in the same body."

"That's only if the first wife was going to die," Ilsa clarifies. "And also only if the dying wife — or *you* — decides to do it. So you could have just decided not to give me your memories. You could have spared us both from being in this uncomfortable position.

Andaleeb looks down at the table, taking a deep breath.

"I... I can't. I *couldn't*. I couldn't let go. I couldn't trust Rohail to make the right decision. I couldn't trust *you*. I had absolutely no control over this whole ordeal. I couldn't control the fact I had gotten cancer, or that I was about to die. And worst of all, I couldn't control the feeling of anger realizing I wouldn't be there for my kids when they needed me. So when they told me I had the *option* of transferring my consciousness to you so I could watch over my kids, while my actual corpse would just decompose, what did you think I was going to say?"

Much like this whole conversation, Ilsa is left at a loss for words. The thoughts of Andaleeb and the pain she must have felt before she died are now circulating in her own mind courtesy of the new chip. It also allows her to empathize with what used to be Andaleeb and her position, but at the same time she's trying to keep her own sense of identity above all.

"No one asked me," Is all Ilsa can say.

"I know," Andaleeb sighs. "I... I'm sorry. I can't imagine what this must be like for you. You shouldn't have to be subjected to my dying breaths as they were. I guess this is just as hard for you as it is for me. And I'm actually dead."

Ilsa takes a deep breath as she looks at the table again, beginning to crack a faint smile that Andaleeb notices.

"What?" Andaleeb asks.

"I just realized," Ilsa remarks as she fingers her hair in place, "I made two mugs of tea but you're not really here. I made tea for a hallucination."

"Ha!" Andaleeb replies. "I'm far more powerful than a hallucination. But yeah, I wouldn't want you wasting good tea. "

"This will take some getting used to."

"Yeah, because imagine having two wives in the head of one. So whether we like it or not, you're going to have to get used to me being literally *in* your head. Though the experience isn't what I thought it would be."

"Yeah, I never realized it would be like this. Being able to talk to you, listen to you, engage with you like this... wait... were you actually *watching* us last night when we... uh..."

"Every blissful moment of it." Andaleeb shakes her head.

"Oh God!"

"It's alright. It's like I said, you make him happy and I'm glad for that. And don't worry, I know I said I couldn't trust you before. But talking to you has made me realize I should give you the opportunity. I'm sure with time you'll be just right for them, for my family. For *our* family. And eventually, I may even take a backseat."

"I hope so. I know this isn't going to be easy, but I think it'll be easier with you around in my head."

"Well, for what it's worth, I'm glad you can trust me too. I wasn't sure we could do this together."

"Yes, we can," Ilsa puts her hands where she thinks Andaleeb's are, seemingly holding them instead of the air. "For Rohail."

"For Rohail." Andaleeb replies.

"For Babur," Ilsa continues.

"For Babur." Andaleeb looks down at their hands.

"For Zoha."

"For Zoha." Andaleeb smiles.

Both Ilsa and Andaleeb smile at each other, as Ilsa finally gets up while picking up the second mug of tea and emptying it in the sink. She washes the mugs and sets them back into the rack and looks back at the table to see there is no one there. She smiles and leaves the kitchen, hopeful and lively.

<u>14</u>

LEGACY

The whiff of rosewater and incense is all that can be felt in the silence. A silence that, though devoid of words, still stirs with the sound of sadness. Still, the continuous sobbing becomes part of the scene itself so much that it doesn't register as any sort of sound at all, like the chirping of swallows on a beautiful morning. And on such a beautiful morning, the sobbing continues in the vast, spartan living room of the house where all women are wearing black and their heads bent over in prayer and contemplation, trying their best not to wail at the sight of the white shroud lying in the center.

For this is a house that has been touched by Death.

And further from them all, inconspicuous to anyone who surrounds the shroud, a man sits at the steps of the living room dressed in a white shirt and pants, also sobbing away at the sight of the shroud. Though his eyes are red with tears, they cannot hide the pain and anguish that encompasses his entire face as he appears to be as distraught as a child who has lost something precious.

"Don't cry, son."

The voice is clear as the last time he had heard it, the friendliest he had heard in his entire life. A voice he had long tried to hear again were it not for the cruel twist of fate life had handed him. He looks over his shoulder to see someone he hadn't seen in years, yet cannot help but be amazed with as much familiarity as one would give to a forgotten item in a drawer that takes you by surprise when they stumble on it; when they least expect it.

And so, he can't help but wonder just why the sight of *Dad* hasn't evoked a more ecstatic response from him. Especially considering he had prayed for this moment for as long as he can remember; that he had begged for just one more moment to be able to see him, to be able to talk to him. Anyone in his place would do the same, especially since his father had passed away many years ago.

"Dad?"

At any other time, he would have been overjoyed at seeing him after all these years, who was also clad in white, in fact in a white shalwar kameez that was starched. Dad had always liked starched clothing, he remembers, but never had he worn white quite as often. Looking at him now, he remembers all the times he had tried to reason with his Creator to give him his father back, and had imagined what his entire adult life would be like if his father were still alive.

"You're here," he asks Dad, "with me?"

"When have I never been with you?"

"There is so much I wanted to tell you. So much I wanted to share with you. My Master's degree; I had to redo some of the subjects, but I got it eventually."

"In Arts," Dad replies. "I know."

He smiles.

"When I brought home my first paycheck, one that I didn't make with the business you were planning to build for us."

"I was very proud of you. I still am."

"When I got married and had children. I would have loved for you to have been a part of their lives. To have taken them to the park every evening."

"I would have liked that, too."

None of that came to pass when he turned nineteen, when his father faced death as he fought for his life in a hospital. It turned that care-free idiot into someone far more responsible, someone more than what he had been. Someone who never planned ahead, who never imagined the worst-case scenario. Before that, the only worst thing that could happen to him was Dad would have killed him if he screwed up again. But once the doctors shook their head, once all the tubes and wires had been disconnected, he had lost that mercy.

And today, after having become a father himself, after losing him all those years ago to the ravages of time; the sight of his father standing over him holding his shoulder and telling him not to cry did not move him enough to get up and hug him after so long. He would very much have liked to do so, finally having gotten an opportunity to embrace the one person who had shaped his life so much in so many ways.

But today, at this very moment, he could not motivate himself enough to even get up from his spot. For the sight in front of him is all that has his attention, his wife and children sitting in the hall with his other relations is all he can think of. His wife, sobbing uncontrollably; his own children trying to comfort her while also breaking down.

He sees them all dressed in white, but they don't see him because he had died just today. All that's left of him is a sad memory that refuses to leave.

"You can't stay here forever," Dad tells him.

"But how can I leave them?" He asked. "They're still so young."

"They'll find a way," Dad answers in his courageous and assuring voice that gave him confidence as a child. "You raised them well enough to come this far. It's now time for them to walk their own path."

"But there's so much still left for me to do," he says as he looks at his wife. "I can't stand to be without her."

"And yet," Dad smiles, "you'll always be with her where it matters most. In her heart."

"And my children?" He asks, his tears beginning to intensify. "They still have their whole lives ahead of them. How could the Creator decide I not play a part in their future?"

Upon hearing this question, Dad lets out a deep breath as his face appears to take on a somber tone. He then sits down next to his son on the steps.

"I asked the same question all those years ago. And I'll tell you exactly what *I* was told: you've done more than what was required of you. You were there for their formative years, turned them into who they are today. You did all this and more. And you've made them ready enough to let go of you. It is their destiny."

"But think about it, Dad," he asks. "Surely you must have felt the same when... when it was your time."

"Yes," Dad answers. "And I suppose I was rather distraught at how Death had made its point. But later I discovered, after seeing you move on and making something of yourself, that it was Life that had made me realize its true value. Life is, well, short and precious. And wonderful, and glorious, and painful. It just *is*. But the thing about life is that it goes on, and has to go on no matter what. The loss of a loved one can only inspire you to follow their example, to carry on and not disappoint them. That is what they would want of you, that is what they would expect of you."

He considers what Dad told him, and a thought couldn't help but strike him.

"You know what my school principal said after you died?" He tells Dad. "He said you were the man I never would be. And he was right. I could never do for my family what you did for us."

"That's because I did what was needed of me. To make sure you were ready for what lay ahead of you. I did it all because I loved you. Because you're my son, and nothing will ever make me want less for you."

Dad leans towards him and puts his arm around his shoulders, holding him warmly.

"And don't worry." Dad smiles. "You've done exactly the same for them too. They will also know all that they are wouldn't have been possible if the Creator hadn't given you their responsibility. For while the Creator is the most benevolent, he chose and blessed you with the obligation of such lovely children. And they would forever be in your debt for being the best you could have been for them."

Looking at his Dad closer to him, feeling his warmth so close and being able to taste the perfume that was his fragrance once upon a time, his tears begin to intensify even more.

"I'm sorry. I'm so sorry!"

Taken slightly aback, Dad looks curiously at his son.

"Sorry? But whatever for?"

"For not being the best son. No, not even close: I was a *terrible* son. I could never be what you wanted me to be, never did what you expected of me. I was a constant disappointment to you at every turn. I turned out totally different from what you wanted."

"You don't have to apologize for anything, my son," Dad tells him gently.

"No, I do! Because I know why you left, why you died so young. It was because of me."

Dad's expression grows from curiosity to concern as his son continues.

"Because I never did well in my studies, because I screwed up everything you ever did for me. No matter what college I went to, what city I lived in, what majors I took, I could never just do as I was told. No, I had to have my head in the clouds and not be concerned with making my own future. And in the process, I caused you so much stress and grief that it killed you inside.

"Now, that's not true..."

"Yes, it is. If I had just tried to be a good and devoted son, I wouldn't have been a total screw-up, and you would still have been here with us..."

"Hush now, stop it!" Dad holds him tighter, his voice a bit stern but not too harsh.

They both share the embrace as they sit in a brief moment of silence, the sobbing of the mourners still masked underneath the fragrance of rosewater and incense.

"Do you know," Dad asks calmly, "what I studied to be?"

"Um," he tries to remember as he sniffles, wiping his tears, "a barrister?"

"Yes, but that's not what I ended up being, is it?"

Still sniffling and wiping his tears, he looks at Dad and smiles when he realizes.

"You went into the performing arts."

"I did." Dad smiles back. "So you tell me, who had his head in the clouds?"

"You're just saying this to make me feel better," he retorts.

"Believe what you like." Dad answers as he removes his arm from his son's shoulders. "It still doesn't change the truth. I forged my own path, and so did you. And for that, you have nothing to be sorry for. Especially not to me."

Once again, Dad had made him feel better and relieved him of one of the biggest burdens he had held onto his entire adult life. Once again, he knew his dad had done for him what no one else in the world would ever do.

"I missed talking to you when you were gone," he tells Dad, "I missed you so much!"

"I know, son," Dad tells him. "I missed you too. Just like I missed your grandfather when he left."

Hearing this, his attention returns to his family sobbing among the mourners, his wife still holding onto their children as they do their best to be her pillars of strength.

"So that must mean," he gulps, "my children will miss me too."

Dad laughs, his signature laugh still as heartwarming as ever.

"Of course! You *are* their father and nothing will ever change that. Not even Death. You run through their veins, live in their every thought. You have groomed them to be the best they can ever be and now they must forge their own path just like you and I. And for all you have done for them, you are and always will be an integral part of their lives till..."

Dad's laughter dies down, his tone remaining solemn but not depressing.

"Till eventually, their own time comes."

Dad sighs as he finishes that last sentence.

"But such is life, my son."

Wiping away the last bits of tears from his face, he finally gets up from the steps and Dad gets up with him too. Looking at his family one last time, he turns around as he and Dad walk side by side together towards the door of the house.

"It's strange," he tells Dad, "I think I saw this whole conversation in a dream. But sometimes I remember you coming to take me, and then I think it was your father coming to take you."

Dad smiles again.

"I know, son. I think I had the same dream, too."

And as they reach the door, he instinctively turns around one more time to look, and sees his children looking towards the door. Looking at him.

"Farewell, my children. See you on the other side."

<u>15</u>

DESOLATION

Shivering under the large shawl she is wrapped around in, under a grey sky with ashen winds blowing at her, she continues her trek onwards on the soil that seems to have been turned over, bumps everywhere as she tries to avoid them. She doesn't remember how she got here, or why she was walking, or where to. Her feet, protected by a pair of sandals that have been worn out from walking, are covered with earth and clay from since the beginning of her trek.

Just how long had she been walking, how much distance had she covered? There was no way to tell the time, as the sky continued to remain that shade of dark grey it had been ever since she started. The sun had yet to make an appearance, yet to nourish this land with its warmth, yet to light up this sky in a blaze of its glorious radiance. Which begs her to wonder, just what could possibly be keeping something as majestic as the sun from pouring its light onto this world?

Or had the sun abandoned this land?

There wasn't even a night sky, the dark black void filled only with stars twinkling just enough to hold aloft everyone's gaze in wonder. The moon, that luminescent ball of soothing white light that had comforted and inspired many a poet to sing in tribute to its beauty and guided many a weary traveler in the darkest of all roads, was conspicuous by its absence to help her as she continued to tread on her path. Tiredness and thirst were somewhere in the corners of her mind, but at the moment she could only think of what she saw... or rather, didn't see.

Turning her head back, she could only see the barren earth with not a tree, not a building, not a whiff of civilization. All she could see were the large bumps in the soil, flattened and disappearing in the winds. Up ahead, she could only see a bare vision of a tree line that she considered to be her destination. That had been her plan all along since she started, to keep walking towards the trees, but they seemed to be moving farther away from her with every step she took. Maybe as she continued to push ahead, she would eventually reach the trees and there would be people there, waiting, walking, laughing.

Living.

Sure enough, after what seemed like hours, she saw someone sitting there facing her. She quickened her pace just to make sure the ground wouldn't slide away from her, that the trees wouldn't run away at her approach, and the man sitting there wouldn't be scared off. She used the last reserves of her breath, panting, gasping as her legs fought against her, the holes in the sandals getting bigger and bigger, the soil trying to slow her down as much as possible. Dauntless though, she finally fell in front of the man, letting out a cry of relief and laughter at finally being able to grab someone. At last she had found a sign of life.

What a pity then he was dead.

Upon pulling herself with the man's shirt, his corpse fell down in the blackened soil, his eyelids permanently ajar and his teeth locked in an eternal grin. If there was a sign of life in him, it had been extinguished long before. Much to her dismay, her last hope after such an immense trek was finally reduced to the ash that kept swirling around her. And with the crushing ferocity of an asteroid impact, her heart felt as if it had been ripped asunder from her chest. Her cries of agony could very well have torn at the ears of anyone around her, if there were anyone there to listen. At the moment, the anguish she let out in her wails could only be carried across the land on the winds.

"Move."

The sound of the word startled her just as much as the hand on her shoulder. Only when she saw it covered in a worn out glove did she see the grizzled man, his hair and beard overgrown and covering his head, his eyes tired and weary with images he had seen almost seared in his irises. Her heart was so crushed at finding the dead man's body that she could not believe there would be any more signs of life. Yet here he was standing in front of her, wearing an old black overcoat and long black boots.

"Move, please."

On hearing his request a second time, she understands and finally slides away. The old man then reaches for the corpse and lifts it over his shoulder, then finally puts it in the nearby wheelbarrow.

"Who are you?" She asks him. "Where are you taking him?"

"There," he answers back, while pushing the wheelbarrow in a certain direction.

She manages to regain her senses as she follows him towards the large mound of soil with a shovel driven into it.

"What are you going to do with him?" She continues her questions.

"What needs to be done."

"What happened to him, how did he die?"

"He's not the only one."

With that, he pauses and turns to look to his left, the woman following the gaze towards another mound she mistakes for more soil. She hesitates as she walks towards it, when she realizes to her horror it isn't soil, but more corpses. More of the dead; men, women, children. The elderly, the infirm, the young and the fit. Some may have left the mortal coil at their own time, some bear the marks of conflict and scars of brutal war. Some look like they feel at ease with their demise, some stare wide-eyed and open mouthed at the terror of their doom. But all of them were most assuredly dead, just like the one she had seen before. The one who the old man now dumped into an open hole where the actual mound of soil lay.

"All of them, what happened to them? How did they all die?"

The old man looked at her, then at the corpses he had pointed to earlier till finally lowering his gaze.

"They all turned on each other. They couldn't stand being in each other's presence. Or they couldn't stand the fact that the others existed."

"But, surely," she ponders, "not all of them could have killed one another."

The old man looks at her, his face expressionless and in a constant state of being weathered.

"*They* all did." He says as he points towards the direction from where the woman had trekked through.

It was only when she looked closely at the path she had traversed - at the bumps along her way that she had taken care to avoid - did she realize the old man had already been there before. That the old man had been busy for quite a long time, as the mounds on her path were evident of the fact. That those blackened mounds of soil were graves as far as the eye could see, spread across in rows and columns of earth dug up upon itself. Buried underneath all the bumps on her path she had been careful not to step on, and others like it all around her were the ones long dead just like the ones she had seen uphill.

And the old man was their gravedigger, burying all of them back to the earth they had once walked upon.

"How many are there?" she sobs, her voice choking with the anguish upon seeing so much desolation and death.

The gravedigger pauses from shoveling the earth onto the corpse he had just dumped. He looks at his handiwork, the endless graves he had been digging and burying all the dead in.

"I thought all of them were," he remarked, "till I saw *you*. I thought none had survived, till you walked up here."

He continues to shovel the dirt, but does decide to ask a few questions of his own now.

"Where did you come from? How did you manage to survive all this?"

The woman turns around to face him, and finally, weary from all the walking, sits down next to the open grave and watches the gravedigger at work.

"I don't know. I remember opening my eyes and found myself somewhere out there. I had no clothes, no roof, nothing. Everything was so cold, everything was biting at my skin. I didn't know it, but I felt bruised all over even though I have no scars or marks. I found this shawl and started to walk. A little ahead, these shoes were there near the mounds, near the... graves. They must have belonged to one of them."

"Must have done," the gravedigger continues to shovel the dirt, not breaking a sweat.

"I remember... children. My children," she smiles as she recalls some happy memories. "They were so playful, so lively. They loved each other so much and would stop at nothing to make each other happy. They were my pride, they were my life. Sometimes though, they would lash out at each other, get angry at the littlest of things. They would be upset whenever the other would take their things or move into their spaces. They found fault in the tiniest of indiscretions and would be upset for who knows how long. My children. My loving, adorable little children. Could they be..."

Her eyes well up with tears as she can't help looking back towards the graves.

"Could they all be buried there?"

"If they aren't, they will be. *None* survived."

"Could they have?" She lashes out. "I had so many of them."

"How many?"

"I don't, I don't know," she replies, hesitantly. "I just remember I had so many of them."

Hearing this, the gravedigger stops, looking at her face once again.

"What did you say your name was?"

"I didn't. My name is..."

Her voice trails off, her eyes looking downwards in contemplation.

"Well?" He inquires. "Do you have a name?"

"I, uh..." she stammers, "I don't remember. But my children, they all called me *mother*."

"Mother?" He inquires, to no answer from her.

"Just like the mother of them all," he continues. "They all had a mother. They kept calling out to her. This world had many a nation, and all of them relied on some figures called mothers for sustenance. That's why they kept chanting *mother-land* over and over again. I remember they were all in a tiff about the others insulting their mother-land, and so on. That's why they fought with each other. I don't remember for how long, but it must have been going on for quite some time."

"Was there a war?"

"It would appear so. A war to end all wars. Then there was another to end that one, and another, and another. The wars kept on trying to end the other; they all tried to kill each other in so many ways. They used metals and liquids, polluted the seas and the air. They ensured the habitats they lived in would be nothing but scorched earth. They would starve till their end and choke from the air that gave them life. The winds would carry the plagues of death to one and all, and all would return to the bottom of their mother-land. Eventually, all that remains is silence."

She listens intently, trying to make sense of all that had taken place. She tries to understand the stories she was hearing, of how everyone had come to hate each other so much so as to be rid of one another. Her mind was trying to grasp the idea of a kind of mutually-assured destruction that ensured no one would ever survive, not even themselves.

"It still doesn't explain how," she pondered and remarked to the gravedigger. "How such a large amount of people, an entire world no less, could be at each other's throats and destroy themselves. Did no one try to talk any sense into the other?"

"They might have, but good sense never prevailed. This world, these dead are evidence of it. Maybe the forces of destruction, the beings that festered chaos proved to be more powerful and were able to reign supreme over their hearts and minds. They tricked them into finding the littlest of faults in the other and to stand at a complete opposite of it. Some believed a faith different to theirs, some believed the same faith but were at two different extremes about it."

The gravedigger looks back over the ashen horizon and then continues.

"Some were suspicious of the ones who came to seek refuge in their lands, believing them to be usurpers in the guise of the persecuted. Some felt it their divine right of superiority to wipe out entire peoples simply because of their ways of life, or even the different colors of their complexion. Some oppressed another gender, while the other gender decided to rise back and decided all of the other gender must be wiped out. To everyone, the others were a scourge on their very beings. And the others just had to go."

"How could they believe all this would be in their best interest? Why couldn't they see they were better and stronger together?"

The gravedigger pauses again, his lips twitch in a kind of a wry smile.

"It is funny," he thought. "They never believed themselves to be capable of it. They always blamed some dark demon, some rival in their own mythologies who exploited their fears and made them do unspeakable things. They claimed it was these demons who controlled them, drove them into believing all these things. That *they* created the urges within them to do harm to their fellow man and paint them as their enemies. Or they told them the others were the demons who would swallow them whole, eat up their children, and desecrate their wives. At the same time, they tempted them to covet their neighbors' assets, to be envious of their success, to lust upon their womenfolk and drove them towards all kinds of unthinkable transgressions."

"Demons," her lips part in a smile that contains sorrow. "They actually believed they were tempted by demons to do their bidding?"

"Whatever they believed in is irrelevant," he replies, finishing up the mound over the corpse. "They're rotting away to give any answers."

The gravedigger looked at the completed grave to his satisfaction as he moved to the next one. Once he sinks the shovel deep into the fresh patch of ground, she lets out a cry of pain.

"Are you okay?" He asks as he continues to dig away.

"Please, please stop doing that." She cries. "It hurts so much."

"What, this?" he inquires as he digs again, noticing her wincing and wailing in pain, as if the shovel were poking at her body.

"I... I don't know why it hurts."

The gravedigger pauses for some time to let her catch her breath, however she winces again as soon as he begins to dig the ground.

"Tell me about your children."

"What?"

"What were they like? What did they do?"

The thoughts began to race into her mind as she began to recall their faces. She remembers how they all had done so much in their lives, how they had become such fine men and women. They had grown into doctors, lawyers, priests and businessmen. Some of them had followed a righteous path, while others had strayed towards the darkness. She realizes she had seen the pattern of their downfall emerging long, long ago, but was too occupied with forgiving them over and over. She had punished them, though; far too many times to count. She had flooded them using the mighty oceans, shaken the very ground they walked upon, unleashed a raging fire to burn away the mischief from them. They relented, and she forgave; and it started all over again.

It occurred to her after the gravedigger was done burying the next body that the pain she was feeling earlier had subsided while she was regaling him with her stories. Even the gravedigger noticed how she no longer felt the pain as he continued with digging another grave, and she kept telling him about her many children.

"Mother," he realized at last. "You *were* mother to them all."

She smiles.

"Yes, I was mother to them all. And now they're all gone. Except... except you."

She now looks at the gravedigger more thoroughly, his haggard attire and woolen cap, his hair and beard grayed of old age, his hands blistered and his face wrinkled. His eyes, those that had seen so much for so long, could only work mechanically as he continued his task.

"Why you? Why are you still here? And why of all things are you burying the dead?"

The gravedigger stops and rests his chin on the handle of the shovel, lost in thought.

"I knew the answer once. I think... I think I woke up one day too and couldn't bear the enormity of this, this desolation. I felt burdened somehow, and knew I had to return these wretches back to the earth from whence they came. After all, it wasn't as if I had anything better to do. And they would do more for the earth under it than over it."

"How long have you been burying them? And who are you?"

"I'm a gravedigger. It's what I've always been doing."

"Even before all this death?" She asks.

He doesn't answer immediately, lost in thought as he was.

"I think... I think I remember..."

"What? What do you remember?"

"A *song*." He replies.

"A song?" She parrots back in surprise.

"It's all I can remember. It's not a very good song. You wouldn't like it."

"Could you sing it?" She inquires.

"Maybe."

And once he finishes digging the new grave and returns with his wheelbarrow carrying another corpse, she can faintly hear the grim melody of his voice. She tries to recall where she's heard the song before, but can't seem to place it. Her children might have played it once, but it would appear she had never paid attention to it.

'Please allow me to introduce myself

I'm a man of wealth and taste

I've been around for a long, long year

Stole many a man's soul to waste'

'And I was 'round when Jesus Christ
Had his moment of doubt and pain
Made damn sure that Pilate
Washed his hands and sealed his fate'

'Pleased to meet you
Hope you guess my name
But what's puzzling you
Is the nature of my game'

Meanwhile the gravedigger - mechanical in his movements as ever - shovels the earth over the grave as he continued to sing in his grim undertone for his sole spectator, who looks curiously at him now. Not just because of the words of the song, but for a brief instant, she thought she saw a glow in his eyes.

A *red* glow.

The End

Check out the following social media pages for more exclusive Damaged content.

https://www.facebook.com/DamagedStories

https://www.instagram.com/masamejo/

www.ingramcontent.com/pod-product-compliance
Lightning Source LLC
Chambersburg PA
CBHW031500160726
47994CB00005B/2120